CONNOR ALEKSEEV

THE GLASS SHADOW

BY

C. R. KELCHNER

BOOK ONE

To Brittany

The Chrysalis

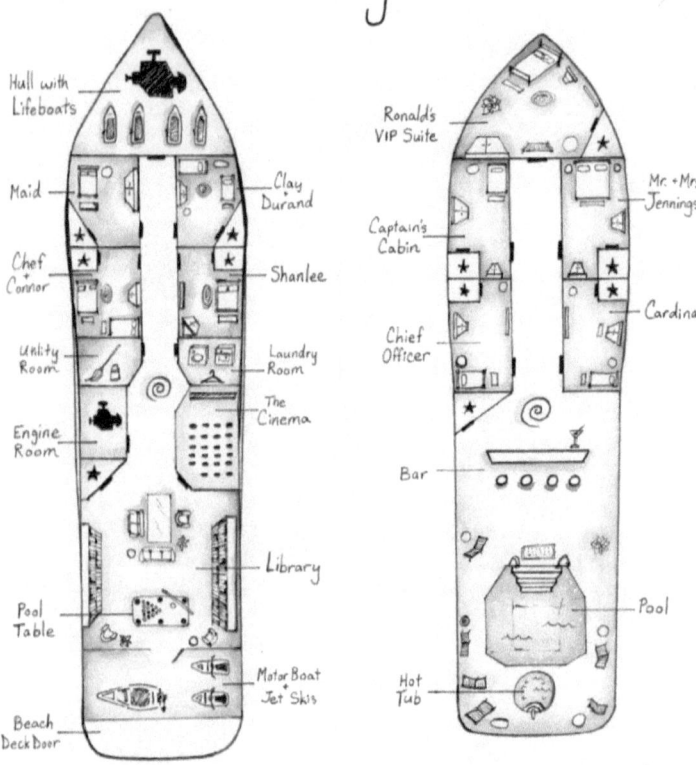

Deck 1

- Hull with Lifeboats
- Maid
- Chef + Connor
- Unility Room
- Engine Room
- Pool Table
- Beach Deck Door
- Clay Durand
- Shanlee
- Laundry Room
- The Cinema
- Library
- Motor Boat + Jet Skis

Deck 2

- Ronald's VIP Suite
- Captain's Cabin
- Chief Officer
- Bar
- Hot Tub
- Mr. + Mrs. Jennings
- Cardinal
- Pool

Key:
- ★ bathroom
- ⊚ Stairs

Samila Designs

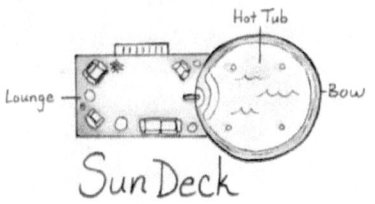

Sun Deck

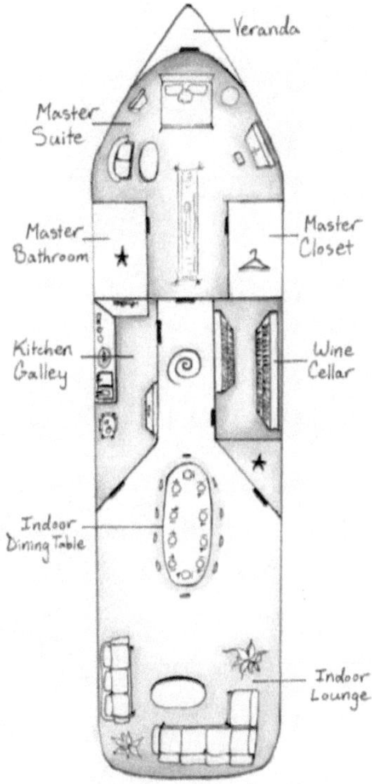

Hot Tub

Lounge

Bow

Veranda

Master Suite

Master Bathroom

Master Closet

Kitchen Galley

Wine Cellar

Indoor Dining Table

Indoor Lounge

Deck 3

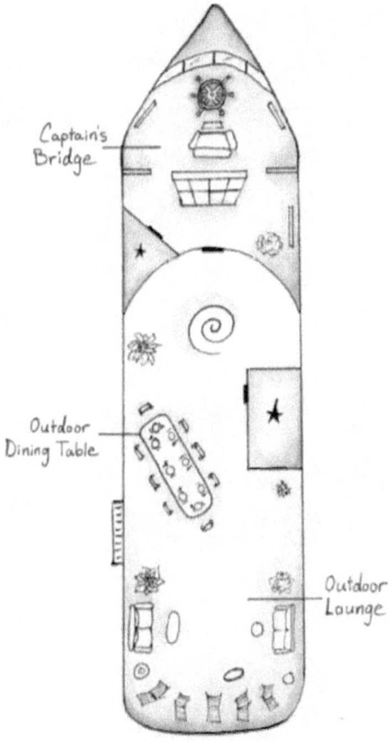

Captain's Bridge

Outdoor Dining Table

Outdoor Lounge

Deck 4

Sanila Designs

1

Little, brown birds liked to walk very close to the waves on the Florida beach and poke their noses in the sand. Even though the salty froth raced after them and sometimes wet their feet, the silly things raced right back to the edge of the receding wave and pecked as much as they possibly could. A freshly washed-up seagull corpse lay where the water couldn't reach it, where the ninety-five degrees sizzled abandoned wet things. But that wouldn't be for a while; the sun was still behind the purple fluff.

A big toe pressed into the damp sand and buried a smooth shell. A drop of the drowning granules flicked up and onto the man's naked knee. His twice-striped indigo swim trunks were enough clothing for any man who knew he was one, or at least that's what Connor Alekseev thought. Or did he? After last night, nothing was for certain except for the fact that he had made a mistake—again.

Like glass with a shadow behind it, the slick beach reflected the sky and its gold, peach, and azure beauty along with the clouds that stretched, free and innocent, while the waves rumbled and roamed over the land they kissed. The sunrise surf had always done this to the sand without any after effect. It was very intimate with this opposite substance; the sand washed in with the salt water, and the salt water seeped into the sand, complementing each other quite well.

"They were right," Connor muttered, his feet settling in the drenched sand. "They were right about me." With a loud cry of frustration he leaped out into the water, slammed his fists against the sea, and dropped low. A cruel wave struck him down and pulled his feet out. Another came and ruffled his hair, tugging more. At least his salty tears mixed nicely with the sea.

Connor sat up and spat. Sighing would now be the only way he breathed, just like before. The sun kept rising and the wind kept blowing as the world continued to turn. He had lived a new life, but now he had made a new mistake.

"How could you be so careless? After only two months!" He fell on his back again, gazing up at the carefree lavender fluff as it listlessly drifted south.

"I can't live here anymore. I have to get out." Connor scraped the sand off his finger. "I have to." He looked up at the sky. "I just need to start a new life. I just need a new pattern. Then I can forget and move on and…" He chuckled, grabbed a handful of sand, and threw it. "And be free."

Connor laughed his self-mocking, thoughtless laugh, the same laugh that caused him to forget himself last night. His white smile was the same, too—the smile that stirred up his willpower to make rash decisions.

The pain came back. "Gaaah!" He groaned and tore at his chest with another long exhale. "I'll escape—this time to a job." With a new confidence and the pain smothered for now, Connor left the beach, rapidly thinking of who to be next.

2

Ronald Jennings considered the restaurant Renfleur New York to be the epitome of fine dining. It wasn't his enormous suit jacket and worn check-signing hand that made him desire elegance tonight. It was his old friend. *What's taking her so long?* he thought. *Curse that rain! If this messes with my plans, then I may as well throw the towel in now.* He wiped his moist hands on the tablecloth and smoothed his tie.

After entering the restaurant, a thin, frail woman in a very expensive black-and-white evening gown made her way to the table. The gown draped over her form like a sheet over a warped coffin.

"It's about time," Ronald whispered under his breath as the woman came up to him. "Orlean! It's great to see you!" He squeezed the bony figure.

"Great to see *you*, Ron." Her jewels rattled and clanged as she sat in the chair that was pulled out for her.

"My, my." The table shook as Ronald scooted his chair in with a great heave of his gargantuan body. "You look great today!" A necessary lie. "Wow! Isn't that the dress you bought in Paris? My word, that was so long ago."

Orlean's eyes attempted to glow, crinkling as she smiled. "Yes, yes, it is. I'm amazed that you remember."

"I could never forget that trip. It had to be the best trip to the City of Light that I have ever been on." He slid her menu away. "I ordered you the special tea and the scallop sandwich. Is that all right?"

"Sounds delicious."

"Here, let me pour you a cup." Ronald doted, jumping up to accomplish the task.

Satisfied with her first sip, Orlean inquired, "Didn't you go to Paris with Marina for your honeymoon, though?"

"We're divorced." He forced a chuckle. "I thought you knew."

"Oh, that's right. I think I did know. Doesn't the thought of France bring back painful memories of her, then?"

"No, not at all," Ronald huffed. "She's quite forgotten in my mind. We never really enjoyed each other. Frankly, I can't even recall one pleasant memory with her."

"Really? Come now, I can tell when you're lying."

"I would never lie to you, Orlean. If I can't be honest with you, then I'm not sure there is a point to my life."

"Ron, that was the sweetest thing I have ever heard you say." She cleared her throat and placed her napkin on a different knee. "I was hoping you would feel this way with me because…" Ronald leaned closer, waiting for the blessed words. "I have been very unhappy lately. In fact, I have been absolutely miserable for the past ten years."

"Oh, Orlean! I am so sorry."

"A decade, Ron. I have been near suicide for a decade. I know it's shocking. The truth is, I am extremely lonely on the *Chrysalis*. The crew never satisfied me. I don't even know how I lived that life for so long. Ron, I need company—real company—not just someone I've hired."

"I will help you in any way I can."

"I knew I could count on you." She smiled weakly, resembling a zebra, starved and parched, wandering aimlessly through a void, hot savanna without companions except for the nibbling flies that buzzed and stole her lifegiving blood. But the zebra did not bother to shake away the pests for she was too tired and far too alone to be angry. She was lost under the sun. "We are sailing for Europe in three weeks, and I was wondering—you don't have to say yes—if you would join me."

His delight was no act this time. "What a tremendous honor! Yes, I will. I would like nothing better than to sail with you on your voyage." His expression melted, and he told her with the semblance of care, "But I'm afraid that won't be enough to make you happy. You need more people—some truly good people. You need to do something for those who would never ask for it themselves or even dream of it. Believe me, charity helps."

"Upon whom should I bestow this tremendous charity?"

"I know just the people. My brother and his family are very, very good people. They have always dreamed of taking a trip to Europe, but the plane fare has never been affordable for them. They finally saved up enough money this year, but my brother used it to help a poor couple. He's a very unusual kind of lawyer. He never asks for anything for himself. Preston and his wife are the most selfless souls I have ever met. They would consider you heaven sent if you could lend them a hand and give them a ride to Europe."

"You really think that will help with my sadness?"

"Yes, I do."

She wrinkled, smoothed, and resmoothed the placemat throughout the remainder of the meal. The food came, the lights flicked off once from the storm and then on again, and finally, during dessert, Orlean Cavenaugh made her decision.

Mrs. Tanya Jennings was a lovely woman with long, straight brown hair and wide hips. She allowed herself to rest, just for a moment, on the living room couch, her mind wandering. *I have a new son now. I'm so glad I finished those adoption forms. What a terrible childhood. I don't know if I could've survived that kind of trauma. Burned. Both of them in the same night. Durand certainly is strong to survive that pain, the poor boy. Now he is such a good boy. He's a new man. I always wanted a son that would read and read like he does. He's so diligent. I was never that diligent at his age. Now I'm raising a boy who's diligent. How wonderful. It's just perfect. He's so mature, but he doesn't interact with people much. I wish he would interact with Clayton. Poor Clay. If only Preston would spend more time with him, then all my troubles would be solved. I love Preston. I can't believe I'm so critical of him. He's the best man in the world…saved those two innocent dears without a second thought. Oh, but Europe! No. How could I be so selfish to want Europe over that beautiful couple's happiness? I can't believe myself. No. I'm so very happy for them. Europe is too vain, anyway…all that gaudy art…*

"Hey, Mom, I'm home." A young woman of Taiwanese descent entered and tossed her backpack on the sofa.

"Hi, Shanlee. How was college?" Tanya rose to her feet and leapt over an empty dog bed to greet her adopted daughter.

"Fantastic! I think at least one person from my debate class will qualify for the national tournament this year. We're really good. I love it." Shanlee smiled, a victorious shine flashing in the edges of her eyes.

"I'm glad you had a good time."

Shanlee began searching for water habitually and entered the kitchen as her mother trod the pristine tiles as well. "I got ninety-seven percent on my paper today," Shanlee stated, removing a glass from the polished cabinet.

Tanya's weary face burst into a vivid grin. "Wow, Shan! That's wonderful! For your Principles of Justice final?"

"Yes."

"You certainly are my prodigy." Smiling with a mother's pride, Mrs. Jennings hugged her adopted daughter. "Not many people get that grade—even those who are twenty-one—but you are nineteen and already on your third year of college. Your hard work is paying off. I'm so proud of you."

Tanya admired her daughter. She had raised a gorgeous young woman who now beamed with overflowing talent and potential. Yes, Shanlee was a prodigy, but more than that, she worked hard at it—harder than anyone.

Shanlee gushed appreciatively. "What do you think Dad will say?"

Tanya cleared her throat, swallowing worry. "Oh, he will bless you and praise you for it, of course. Anyway, hey, why don't you stay home from youth group tonight so we can relax and watch a movie? You deserve it."

"I can't, Mom. I have to stay true to my commitments." She glanced at the microwave's clock. "Yikes! I'd better leave now, or I'll be late." She grabbed her denim-cased Bible and raced out the door. "See ya!"

Tanya watched Shanlee's car drive away from the window. *She works so hard. I miss her already.* Since she was already clothed in practical attire—sandy-brown khakis and a simple shirt—Tanya decided to go outside and do some yard work.

The dry heat whirled around her and the powerful sunlight blared as she walked out into her back yard. She placed sunglasses over her eyes and looked out at the vast, beige desert stretching far. A gray peak in the McCullough Range displayed its rocky face, a face that blushed with triumphant pink when the dominant sun bestowed its gift of evening light. She bent down and began spreading dusty pebbles around a cactus. The soaring chorus of a song blew through her mind, Shanlee's favorite song: *I am defined in Jesus. Your love is the water for my soul. Christ is my identity. You, O Lord, are my strength.* She prayed for more time to spend with her daughter.

Her cell phone rang.

"Hello, Preston."

"Hello, my Tanya." Her husband sounded happier than usual. "I have some very good news."

"Okay. What's the news?"

"I got a call from my brother, Ronald, today."

"After all these years? What did he want?"

"It was quite strange. He offered us a trip to Europe on a yacht owned by Lady Orlean Cavenaugh. She wants some company."

Tanya gasped with exuberance. "You're joking?"

"I investigated the offer and looked over our finances one more time. The trip is legitimate. If we drive to the departure city in New York, I think we can afford to go."

"What? Really? Oh my word, Preston! Is it true? We're going to *Europe*?"

"Yes, as long as you approve."

"Of course! If you approve then I approve." She giggled and touched her mouth with three fingers. "I can't believe it! Where all would we go?"

"Lady Cavenaugh has a full itincrary planned out. Gibraltar, Madrid, Sicily, Athens and Crete. I was considering separating from her plan and taking our family inland more…"

As Preston articulated his vision for their future vacation, Tanya wondered how excited her children would be when she told them. *I can't wait to see their faces! Durand will peel his eyes away from his books and finally smile; Clay will certainly give me a big hug and maybe even shout. I can't wait to see Shanlee take a break from her busy schedule! This will definitely bring our family together!*

U nder the enormous dome of Saint Peter's Basilica, Cardinal Sabino Verdone strolled through the ornate rows. A second cardinal in ceremonial red and white approached him.

"*Buongiorno*, Sabino," said the man, with a courteous bow of the head. "I hear you are taking a trip?"

"Yes, Angelo. I have just come here to pray about it."

"Why are you hesitant?"

Sabino pondered for a moment while they passed a towering marble pillar. "Forgive me, Angelo. It is a family matter. My sister, Orlean, has led an unsavory life. She took advantage of her privileges as the widow to the late Lord Cavenaugh. Yet, now she has invited me to join her on a transatlantic voyage."

"You are concerned about her influence, no?"

"Bad company is a force of corruption," Sabino replied. "However, I do want to see her again. We are both getting old."

"You must go. After Joseph spent many years in Egypt, did he not meet his brothers once again?"

"An excellent point." Sabino stroked his chin with his thumb and forefinger. "However, please pray with me about it. I have a cold fear that this voyage is not what it seems."

3

The Past

Beneath the dimming twilight sky, fourteen-year-old Connor searched the busy crowd on the Fourth of July. People packed in like sardines in the line for the hot dog grill. Volunteers stuffed festive paper bags with buttery popcorn, handing them out as fast as they could. But where were his friends? Where were the Stonewells?

And then he felt a tap on his shoulder.

"There you are! Welcome!" It was Mrs. Andalucía Stonewell, the friendliest homeschool mom Connor had ever met. She smiled proudly as she greeted him, as if Connor were one of her own.

"Wow, you startled me!" said Connor.

"Sorry. Next time I'll say 'Boo!' " She roared with laughter, her wavy black and auburn hair bobbing around. "Oh, there's Blake. Come on!"

Blake was leaning against a brick wall, watching the throng like a cowboy observing a herd of cattle.

He was tall and rugged with compassionate amber eyes. "Hey, Con. Happy Independence Day! Glad you could make it. Did you ride your bike here again?"

"Yep, like always."

"I'm very impressed," Mrs. Stonewell commented. "You're probably getting into great shape. Oh! There's Norman and the girls."

They joined three other members of the Stonewell family on a ledge that was sure to have a great view of the fireworks. Clad in black slacks and a patterned gray button up, the brawny Mr. Norman Stonewell was sitting patiently, his two tween daughters coloring in their books.

"Wait. Where's Diego?" Mrs. Stonewell fretted about her second-oldest son.

"He's getting your lemonade," said Norman.

"Oh, that's right." Mrs. Stonewell roared with laughter again.

"Mom, you worry too much," said Diego as he walked up and handed out several cups of strawberry lemonade. Mrs. Stonewell put her hand on Diego's shoulder, relieved to see her family all together—plus their special guest.

The group settled into their various positions as they waited for the fireworks to begin. Connor chose a spot beside Blake on the ledge. "Hey, Blake, so if you were to have any job in the world, what would it be?"

"I've always wanted to be in the military," Blake answered.

"Oh, cool. I guess that's why you're going to Junior ROTC now, huh?"

"Yeah. You should join us sometime, Con!"

"Hmm, interesting thought." Connor crunched a salty kernel of popcorn. "How are you able to manage JROTC, schoolwork, and your part-time job?"

"It's a lot, but having my own truck helps," Blake responded.

"Oh, here's another one," said Connor. "If you were to travel to any country in the world, what country would it be?"

"Probably England."

"Nice. I'd love to go to England too!" Connor washed down the popcorn with a chug of lemonade. "I just thought of another one. If you could build a house from any material except wood, what material would you choose?"

Blake thought for a moment. "I don't know, man. Maybe brick? Good grief, you sure ask a lot of questions."

"I'm just trying to understand the world," Connor retorted.

"I'm going to have to give you a nickname because of it, though." Blake smirked. "I'll call you Parrot."

"What! But parrots are copycats."

Blake chuckled. "I think it fits."

"All right then, sir," Connor said in a sassy tone. "I'm going to call you a bird name too! Like Eagle."

"Eagle? That's a compliment. Thank you."

"You're welcome." Connor became a bit more serious. "Honestly, though, this is really nice to celebrate with you guys tonight." He glanced at Mrs. Stonewell, wondering what she would think of his next comment. "Homeschooling is great and all, but it's kind of hard to have a social life."

Mrs. Stonewell's brown eyes glistened with a hint of reconsideration.

"Things will get better soon," said Blake. "You really should visit JROTC. Have you ever thought of being in the military?"

"Not much before now, but I guess I'll have to change that."

Explosions of purple, azure, and scarlet peppered the sky like sprinkles on a cake. As a patriotic tune rang through the air, Connor felt supremely content—refreshed, peaceful, wanted, and loved.

After the fireworks display ended with a round of applause, they flocked out with the rest of the crowd. Connor stopped at his bike and started putting on his helmet.

"You're not going to ride your bike home tonight, are you?" Mrs. Stonewell asked.

"Sure. I know the way." Connor smiled confidently.

"Oh no, please don't. It's so late. Norman!" She turned to her husband.

Mr. Stonewell faced Connor. "Bring your bike. We'll give you a ride home in Blake's truck."

"Really? Thank you! That would be a huge help."

4

The sun lifted above New York Harbor, pouring light upon the rested world, eager to grin on busy people. City dwellers everywhere roused from their slumbers, scrambling around apartments and hunting for devices and wallets. It was a day to make not only money but intentional changes and key first impressions. Little doves watched the boat twinkling in the morning rays while they cooed and tutted on skyscraper ledges.

Connor Alekseev stood on the deck of the *Chrysalis* yacht, a boat that was not for him; it was for the rich and famous. Connor had striking sky-blue eyes and combed light-brown hair. At age twenty-three, his clean, angular features still retained the boyish quality of a teenager.

Connor had just finished training for his new job as a steward on the *Chrysalis*—the most luxurious floating vessel he had ever trod upon. The yacht had five levels, ten bedrooms, fourteen bathrooms, a pool, two hot tubs, a library, a large wine cellar, a bar, a cinema, indoor and outdoor dining tables, and several lounge areas. It was staffed with a maid, steward, chef, captain, and chief officer. The *Chrysalis* was equipped to be a floating soirée.

The Jennings family had arrived early in a minivan. The mother with long brown hair laughed giddily, touching her analytical husband. A Caucasian boy clumsily got out of the back seat as an African American boy clung to a young woman of Asian descent, who was marveling at the view. Had she seen him? Connor decided to go down and help the maid with the final preparations.

He entered a stateroom on deck onc, the lowest deck. The Arabic maid, Najah Hasan, quietly nodded to him and directed her demure bronze face toward the sheets she was smoothing. Connor leapt to her aid, efficiently unfolding a blanket and placing it on the bed.

"That's the last one," he remarked. "Is there anything else you need?" She shook her head so fast and slight it might have only been a twitch. Connor looked at Najah curiously. "Did you enjoy your time in New York City last night?"

For the first time Najah spoke to him, keeping her gaze fixed downward. "No. The people focus on things that don't matter."

Connor watched the nervous woman continue to smooth, tuck, and resmooth the blanket again and again as if waiting for him to leave the room. *The poor, frightened girl,* he thought and placed his hand on her shoulder. He began to say something, but before he could, Najah darted away from his touch and brushed her sleeve violently where his hand had been. She stared at him suspiciously.

"I'm sorry." Connor was bewildered by her quick movements. "I didn't mean to frighten you."

She continued to stare.

"I only wanted to help you."

The woman stepped farther away, holding her steady, wide-eyed gaze, and replied, "No, it is fine." She turned and headed for the door. "I must get another towel for this bathroom. The guests are already arriving." With that, she swept out, leaving Connor standing with an extra towel in his hand.

Orlean Cavenaugh's thin dress fluttered in the wind like the colorful butterflies would if freed from the embroidered green silk. Her spotted face managed a long, straight smile while she greeted her guests. Ronald was standing beside her. "Mrs. Tanya Jennings, it is so nice to meet you. Mr. Preston Jennings, what a pleasure. Are these your children?" She surveyed the two teenagers and the child with adoration and a tilted head.

They smiled politely, saying, "Thank you" and "Yes, it's nice to meet you, too."

Orlean turned to her crew. "This is the ship's captain, Thomas Neals, and the chief officer, Brock Minton." They shook hands with each of the members of the family while extending their greetings. "And this is my chef, Xenon Leveque." He smiled with exaggerated vivacity for each of them and bowed very low. Connor came out the door and across the wooden deck, approaching the group. "Please look around the yacht as much as you like. I would show it to you myself, but I have another guest to greet," Orlean told the family. When she saw Connor approaching, she turned to him. "This is my steward, Connor Alekseev. He will show you to your rooms and answer any questions you might have about the ship."

"Please follow me," said Connor. "Actually, Lady Cavenaugh just hired me, so I am about as new as you are…"

The wind blew, hushing the voices and dimming the smiles as Orlean gazed out at the city. Ronald turned to her affectionately. "Do you want me to greet him with you?"

"No, thank you, Ron. I must do this alone."

Respectfully, Ronald left Orlean to wait alone.

Orlean was weak—too weak to hold her head up and too weak to even stand. She grabbed the closest sunchair and fell into the cushions. She scraped her side against the edge and winced. Her hands were heavy and her arms were limp as she tried to recall the last time she had seen her brother. Hazy clips of childhood images leapt in and out of her mind in split seconds. The bright Italian sun. The emerald vineyard with the amethyst jewels of the ripe red grapes, ready to be pressed into wine. The laugh of a boy once familiar but now a stranger known long ago. She tried to imagine the sound of the laugh, but that memory was fleeting. It seemed to be the only memory she had of him, a boy blissfully laughing on the rolling hills in the Tuscany sun. Sabino always had a joy and a curiosity for spiritual things that Orlean had never possessed. She wanted it once and tried to be a good Catholic child, but Sabino was so much better at being spiritual that she abandoned the effort and followed her passions. It was the first step that got her to where she was, sitting weak and frail in a wooden chair on a lonely yacht—with melanoma.

The harsh diagnosis pinched her mind. Stage four cancer—death waiting around the corner. Orlean would never forget the way the doctor informed her of the news, propping up his clipboard like a shield. He said the cancer had spread to several lymph nodes throughout her body. Even if they operated immediately, it wouldn't increase her chances of survival. If only she had sought treatment earlier. No matter how she tried to avoid it, death would reach her soon. How could she sympathize with her brother's life during all this?

The limousine pulled up and stopped. Orlean came back to the present and nervously watched the vehicle. The driver retrieved the bag from the trunk and opened the backseat door. An elderly man in a suit emerged and thanked the driver for his assistance, handing him a tip.

Is this my brother? Is this Sabino? Orlean asked herself. She could hardly believe it. He appeared to be just another short, clean-shaven old man of her generation. Yet Orlean could see that he was a good man. He seemed to be completely transparent; she could tell that he had a pure heart just by watching him, the way he shook the driver's hand, the way he gazed up at her. Sabino appeared to want nothing but pure happiness for others.

"Hello, Orlean. It's been a long time."

"Yes, Sabino, it has—far too long." She smiled with true appreciation. "Come, brother, I will show you to your room."

"This is the library." Connor motioned to the bookcases as he gave the Jennings family a tour of the yacht. He looked over the family: Preston Jennings was a thin, worn man with an emotionless face and small glasses. Tanya Jennings was a lovely, brown-haired woman with wide hips, cheerful and giddy. She must be very excited about the trip. Connor could immediately tell that the three children were adopted. The youngest was an African American boy, probably in third or fourth grade, with enthusiastic eyes that were full of dreams. The second youngest was a curly-haired teenager with pale skin and thick glasses that emphasized his apparent discomfort. He gawked at everything. Connor wanted to say, "It's okay, dude. You're fine."

The oldest caught Connor's attention the first moment he saw her. She was like a beautiful waterlily with just the right amount of lavender petals. Her shoulder-length black hair framed her oval face like a painting. She glowed with a good nature that calmed Connor and made him feel happier somehow.

"Wow," Tanya commented, obliviously stepping on the transparent glass floor. "Breathtaking."

"Lady Cavenaugh has a vast selection of movies as well as books. Feel free to come here, pick out whatever you want, and bring it back to your room. The movies are in the cinema." He pointed to a black doorway.

Shanlee turned to Connor and asked him pleasantly, "Have you ever been to Europe before?"

"Yes, I've been to Italy," said Connor. "But it was only a short trip to Rome and a few other cities. The itinerary Lady Cavenaugh has planned definitely tops all the vacations I've been on: Gibraltar, Madrid, Sicily, Athens and Crete. It will be amazing."

"Sounds like you're almost as excited as we are." Shanlee smiled teasingly.

Connor was pleased by her friendly attention. "Yes, I think so. Hey, I heard that you guys flew in from Nevada. What town?"

"We're from a city just outside of Las Vegas, called Henderson," Shanlee answered.

"Really?" Connor grinned. "That's where I grew up! Wow, small world!"

The group continued their tour, while Shanlee and Connor chatted about the city of Henderson.

With all thirteen people aboard her, by the hand of Captain Neals, the *Chrysalis* left the marina, inching away at first then gaining speed. The yacht passed enormous barges loaded with multicolored containers, under two bridges with many rushing cars, and finally by Ellis Island and the Statue of Liberty. Staffed, stocked, and polished, the *Chrysalis* was ready for a transatlantic voyage.

5

The city grew farther and farther into the horizon as the *Chrysalis* propelled through the swells in the ocean. It rocked some, a trail falling behind like a past experience recalled in wondering, lofty moments. The little flaws in the trail caused by intruding waves were like mistakes that you notice only when you look back.

The noon sun cast pleasing tingles of warmth on any skin exposed to it; the back of Shanlee Jennings's neck was affectionately tanned by these rays while she lay on a deck chair by the pool. A seagull listlessly floated through the air under white fluff.

At noon Connor made his rounds on the pool deck while balancing a tray of food and drink on his right hand. He wore a white short-sleeved polo uniform. As he shielded his eyes from the bright sun, he noticed Shanlee in the deck chair. "Enjoying your book, Miss Jennings?"

In her one-piece violet swimsuit, Shanlee turned over and looked up at him, shading her eyes with her hand. "Yes, I am. Did you bring me lunch?" Her eyes glistened with acceptance.

"Yes," he replied. He made sure to use his deep, soothing voice. Women always liked that. "The chef made some excellent broiled lobster with orange mango salsa. Here is your ice water."

"Thank you." She took a sip, set the glass back on the tray, and turned to continue reading. Connor waited for a moment.

Shanlee caught the hint. She closed her book and bounced up on the deck chair, cross-legged as if sitting on a trampoline. "Tell me about your trip to Rome. That sounds absolutely thrilling! We might go there and I would just love to hear about it."

Emboldened, Connor glanced over his shoulder and perched on the chair beside her. "It was after I graduated from college. I went on a trip to Italy with my family. Just a couple weeks. We went to Rome, Venice, and Florence. If you make it to Rome, you have to see the Sistine Chapel and the Colosseum. You'll feel transported to a different era."

"Wow! Your family treated you? How wonderful!" Shanlee declared. "What are they like?"

"Who? My family?"

"Yes."

"Oh, my parents have always been very supportive and encouraging." Connor's throat suddenly felt dry. "What about you? What is your family like?"

Shanlee interlaced her fingers, tucking them beneath her chin. "Mom and Dad are wonderful. They adopted me when I was a baby. Mom is super encouraging and affectionate. And I do enjoy time with my brothers too, especially Clayton. I'm just super busy these days, being in college and all. But my professors gave me permission to step away for two weeks. This vacation is the best thing that could have happened to us."

As Connor listened to Shanlee, he watched her smile and move her hands, like a performance of graceful ribbons. He was smitten. "Hey, so, do you like dancing?"

"What? Dancing?" She burst into laughter. "I've never danced in my life."

Connor sprang to his feet, smoothing his white polo. "No problem! I used to be a dance instructor." He extended his hand. "Would you like a lesson?"

Shanlee squinted at him, trying to examine his expression as the waves splashed and the engine rumbled. "But there's no music."

"I can fix that." Connor withdrew his phone and quickly played an amorous tune from the forties. "How about now?"

Shanlee's chest rose and fell, and she suddenly jumped up. "Okay. Why not? I'm on vacation."

"That's the spirit." Connor stood as tall and confident as he could, ignoring the impulse to look over his shoulder again. "First, we start with our hands. For swing dancing, the girl points her hands down, kind of like a bunny, and the guy's hands are like a fence that the bunny hops over."

Laughing, Shanlee put her hands into a goofy bunny pose and Connor held up his hands flat in front of him. She wrapped her fingers around his. Connor lightly rubbed her soft fingers.

"What now?" Shanlee asked.

"Now, you mirror my pose as I step to the right and then back to the—"

"Connor!" called the voice of Lady Cavenaugh.

He sighed and turned around. "Yes?"

"No!" She shook a disapproving finger from the deck above.

"Maybe I should get back to my book," said Shanlee.

Reluctantly Connor dropped her hands. "Maybe I should get back to being a steward. Can I do anything else for you before I go?"

Shanlee smiled mischievously. "Yes, you can. I want you to have a wonderful day."

He chuckled. "That should be easy enough. I already got to dance with you."

Connor set the plates onto the large mahogany dining table on deck three. The wine glasses rang a flawless purity as they landed on the glossy wood. He trod the orange bird-of-paradise flowers, embroidered in the clean carpet beneath his feet, and carefully placed the polished forks. He set the water, the bread, and the napkins. When all was done, the table was prepared for the guests.

Right before they entered, Connor remembered the centerpiece and placed it on the table. He noticed a sliver of blue paper fall from the flower display, but he didn't pay attention. Lady Cavenaugh must have put it there.

"How do you like the squid, Preston?" Orlean Cavenaugh inquired from her position at the head of the table. She smiled with pleasure at the delighted sounds of her guests as they savored the rich delicacies.

"Excellent, ma'am. Very tasty." Everyone agreed with nods. Orlean enjoyed their plaudits much more than she expected, and from such a little thing as dinner. She crinkled a smile around her eyes, sipping a champagne she had purchased from Marseille, France.

"I must tell you all." She started to cut another piece of the herb-crusted escargot as the seven people watched her. "I have never had such good and considerate guests before on the *Chrysalis*. No one has ever been so truly kind as you have been." She grinned vividly at everyone.

They smiled modestly and thanked her.

Preston Jennings started a conversation with his brother about a recent oil spill and how much damage it was causing in the Gulf of Mexico. Tanya became very grave and said earnestly, "Those poor workers on the coast. They will go bankrupt here soon. And what will they do then? How will they feed their families? It's horrible."

Orlean was ready to jump into the relevant conversation. "Yes, it's awful. I was going to sail in the Gulf this year until the oil spill happened. Right from the start, I knew it was going to cause this much trouble. Therefore, I planned my trips far away from it."

Ronald Jennings picked up the conversation, his burly neck condensing and his eyebrows low. He was almost too fat to fit in the chair. "This is going to harm the oil industry. Shipping oil will get more expensive and gas prices will rise…"

As the other adults continued analyzing the matter, Orlean observed how Shanlee eagerly listened to the discussion. *She's so beautiful,* she thought. *I would give anything to look like that. The sheltered, naïve girl doesn't know what she has.* Shanlee's black hair was perfectly straight and silky, and her violet earrings sparkled when she turned her head. Her white dress had delicate folds around the neck. *Where did this poor girl get such a beautiful dress? It would look hideous on me, but she really pulls it off.* Orlean hated Shanlee for being gorgeous and innocent at the same time.

Shanlee's eyes noticed something beneath the centerpiece. *What's she looking at?* Orlean's heart panicked when she saw the small piece of blue paper. *Oh no! Not imperfection! Who put that there?* She was furious but forced herself not to show it.

The boy with curly hair and thick glasses tilted his head awkwardly and the African American boy snickered at him, causing the other's pale cheeks to turn pink with embarrassment. *What were their names again?* Orlean strained to remember. *The white boy is Durand, but who is the black boy? Clayton! That's right. I hope he makes it through life decently, rather than stumbling around like so many of his kind. I'll just have to give his parents some money for his education. Yes, that will surely help.* She felt like a good person for having the thought.

"They are almost ready for dessert," Connor told the chef while he peeked out of the kitchen door.

Xenon Leveque chortled in amusement. "Did the pigs enjoy their slop?" He jerked up his tan Mediterranean head.

Connor couldn't understand why he would say something like that about his own specialty. He shook his head slightly. Xenon was the strangest chef he had ever met; he found a large amount of amusement in things that most would consider disgusting or horrible.

"Have you seen the Asian girl?" Xenon asked with a lusty grin in his white goatee.

"Yeah. What about her?" Connor didn't like his tone.

"She's a looker, boy. When I got bored with my wives and mistresses, I would get with girls like her. You should sleep with her. If you don't, I will."

Connor hated the chef for saying this and didn't even bother to respond. He had thought about women in that way before, but Shanlee was different. She was good. *I'm going to make sure the chef gets nowhere near her,* Connor promised himself.

Captain Thomas Neals passed by in his finest white uniform heading for the table. Connor wondered why the elderly man appeared constantly sad. He sank into his strides without joy or excitement, as if he were performing a funeral procession.

Orlean noticed the captain standing in clean form with his hands behind his back. His sharply trimmed gray mustache added to his disciplined demeanor. She brought the table to silence with a slight touch of her spoon on her water glass. "Excuse me, my most gracious guests, but please help me welcome my wonderfully skilled and experienced sea captain, Thomas Neals."

The captain bowed his head appreciatively and took his place at the foot of the table.

"You are just in time for dessert, Thomas." She nodded to Connor, who had the tray already in hand. He set each of the plates before the guests as he cleared.

"We were just talking about the oil spill and how problematic it is," Preston Jennings stated, addressing the captain. "What do you think, sir?"

His face went grave again as he swallowed an immensely sweet and savory bite of the passion fruit tartlet. "I think we deserve it," he answered simply.

This did not go over well with the others, who had just agreed that it was economically harsh in the present day. Lady Cavenaugh cleared her throat and started on the dessert, changing the subject. "My, this is so delicious. I must tell Xenon my chef that he outdid himself."

"I think you dropped this." Shanlee handed Connor a fork that had fallen on the floor when he finally came to her. Connor had been watching the reactions of the people at the table and had slipped into clumsiness.

"I'm so sorry." He set the plate in front of her. By now all the eyes in the room were on him as he stood to say the appropriate words. "I'll get you another one."

"If you must," Shanlee commented as if she didn't care in the least if the fork had touched the ground but was allowing Connor to take it for his benefit. She sent him a soft smile. Connor felt a strong affinity for Shanlee as he walked back to the kitchen, bewildered by her carelessly forgiving attitude.

The guests enjoyed the meal tremendously, and so had their hostess. But soon the hour became late, and Mrs. Jennings had to put her children to bed. Starting to leave with her, Preston Jennings said goodnight, and so did Captain Neals and Cardinal Verdone. But after the cardinal told his sister to sleep well, he noticed the small piece of blue paper in the decorative flower display, thinking simply, *Hmm…it looks like a caterpillar.*

6

"Do you agree with the captain's response?" Preston Jennings asked his wife as he dabbed his face with a vetiver scented hand towel in their oceanview stateroom.

Tanya looked at her husband with surprise. "Oh no, the oil spill is horrible. I don't think Americans deserve to deal with that. But what do you think, darling?"

Preston turned off the light and crawled into the king-size bed with his wife. "I'm not sure I disagree with him." As their eyes adjusted to the dark, a streak of moonlight became visible, and they both stared out the glass door which led to the balcony. "America has fallen away from God. The old testament describes many harsher consequences on rebellious civilizations. For example, the sudden change of languages at the Tower of Babel or the numerous plagues in Egypt. Even the chosen people of Israel were subjected to harsh captivity under the empire of Babylon, then Persia, and eventually Rome. Does that change your mind?"

Tanya was confused by the question. It seemed perfectly logical the way Preston explained it, as things always did when he talked. She thought of her sister who owned a small hotel on the coast of Alabama. How could she agree that judgment was right when it would hurt the people she most loved? Everyone she knew would be terribly affected if absolute judgment fell on her cherished country. Without thinking of what to say, three words jumped out of her mouth, "I don't know."

"His statement reminded me of something else," Preston continued. "His words 'I think we deserve it' were the exact words a couple said in a case I was working on last month. They were prosecuting their daughter for having her unborn baby removed. They said the defending lawyer told them that the sentence would be just as painful for them as it would for their daughter. Can you believe that? Parents suing their own daughter. She was eighteen and left her parents to live with her boyfriend at sixteen. Even though it sounds unjust for the parents to sue their daughter, I agree with them."

"You think they were right to sue their own daughter?" Tanya replied, shocked.

"No, not to that extreme. I think the parents should have forgiven her. But I agree with them that destroying the unborn is one of the worst forms of murder and absolutely deserves a harsh punishment." He sighed in the dark. "It's horrible. Killing a baby before it even has a chance to live. That is one of the most precious stages of life when the baby is first conceived and inside the mother."

They were silent as Tanya's heart thumped in her temples. She remembered the "yes" she had said long ago at sixteen. The simple unthinking "yes" she had told the nurse who asked her the question, "Do you want it removed?" She remembered the way the nurse had put it, the problems that would have been caused if she hadn't said yes, and the way the father had utterly rejected her when she told him she was pregnant. The circumstances were so very difficult. She felt the guilt and the wrong in what she was thinking and immediately hated herself for it. *I'm sorry, Lord. I'm so, so sorry. I didn't mean that,* she prayed silently. Tanya hesitantly opened her eyes and saw darkness. She felt worse than before, unable to forgive herself for murdering her own child.

She knew it was murder. No matter how she reasoned with herself over the years, deep down she always knew the yes had been murder. As Preston had said, killing the unborn was one of the worst types of murder. Then she must be the worst type of murderer. How could a person get to heaven if they had denied life to their own child?

"Um, Preston?" she said in a small voice.

"Yes, dear?"

"I'm going to go out on the deck for a minute. Will you excuse me?"

"Yes, of course. Are you all right?" That question, in her husband's concerned voice, almost uncovered the truth and exposed her completely—but she didn't let it.

"Yes, yes, I'm fine." She forced a laugh, which sounded far more like a hiccup than anything else. "I just would like to go look at the moon. That's all. Sleep well, darling." She gave him a peck on the cheek and went for the door.

"Enjoy the moonlight," Preston remarked, resting flat on the bed with his arms crossed.

Tanya slid open the glass door and closed it tightly. The moon was halfway in the sky now, its light shining brightly in dominance and power like the God who made it.

Wait, she prayed, *I'm not that bad of a person. Lord, look at all the good things I've done and all the charities and the children and husband I have served with every breath in my body.* She gazed up at the silver circle and felt nothing but stern reproach. The moon was a spotlight exposing the criminal—Tanya Jennings. She suspected that her good deeds had not been enough to atone for her sin. She felt naked and unable to cover herself.

On the deck chair adjacent to Tanya, Cardinal Sabino Verdone was also gazing at the moonlight. The reflections on the water were quick little brushstrokes, pearly touches tracing back to the source. The clouds were fluffed by a different brush dipped in a choice, dark sapphire. The moon itself was a precious ivory pigment, fair as the beauty of heaven, a small glimpse of the city of God. The sky was a glorious painting, by the Creator himself, and so much more beautiful because of it.

The cardinal turned his head to the left and noticed Mrs. Jennings exit the door and sit in a chair. She fixed her gaze on the moon. Sabino waited a minute and decided to make conversation. "It's a beautiful night, isn't it?"

Startled, Tanya looked to her right and saw the old man, serenely resting in his chair. He was still dressed in a full suit. "Oh, yes, it is."

"Did I startle you?"

"Yes, but that's all right. I'm sorry, what was your name? I know we have been introduced, but I can't remember."

"My name is Sabino Verdone, and I am a cardinal in the Holy Catholic Church."

"That's right. I apologize for my forgetfulness. Lady Cavenaugh is your sister, correct?"

"Yes, she is." They both stared silently at the moon for a moment.

"Excuse me, sir," said Tanya. "Can I ask you a theological question?"

"Yes. I would be happy to answer any question concerning our Lord's kingdom."

Tanya brought all of her long brown hair over her left shoulder, as if reaching for a comforting object. "If a person had done something horrible a long time ago, but for the rest of their life they tried to be a good person, do you think God would let them into heaven?"

"There is only one thing that can wash away sin," the cardinal answered.

"Yes? What is that?"

"The blood of Jesus."

"Hmmm," Tanya replied, as if she had never before heard this answer. "And how does someone get truly washed by the blood of Jesus?"

"You must make him your Lord."

Tanya released her hiccup laugh. "I suppose you've guessed that I'm talking about myself, haven't you?"

Sabino shrugged. "All people have sinned. Blessed are those who acknowledge it."

"But what if I still feel like God is mad at me?" she asked.

The cardinal stroked his chin with his forefinger. "Let me put it this way. The moment after death will be like a court trial. And we will be the ones on trial. If we try to advocate for ourselves, we will fail. The only way to be acquitted of our sins is if we have a very specific attorney—Jesus Christ, the true Messiah. Only he can effectively defend us from judgement."

A faint, "Oh," jumped out as her reply. Tanya grasped her hair with both hands. "Very well put, sir."

The cardinal noticed her obviously troubled heart because it was written as clearly on her face as the face of Mary in the *Madonna della Pietà* sculpture in Rome. "We have a tradition in the Catholic Church where a person goes and confesses to a priest. In confession, you can talk openly about the nature of what it is you have done."

"Talk about it? Openly?" Tanya recoiled at the idea. "I'm not sure I'm ready for that. But thank you for your encouraging words. They are greatly appreciated."

"You're very welcome. But please excuse me. I think it is time for me to go to my stateroom." He began to walk inside but suddenly halted. "Oh, if you ever decide that confession would be helpful for you, I would qualify as a priest. You can confess to me."

"I will keep that in mind," said Tanya pleasantly. "Thank you very much."

"Goodnight, Mrs. Jennings."

"Goodnight, Mr. Verdone."

Watching the moonlight glisten on the vast ocean, Tanya Jennings was stricken by a great desire for her husband. In that moment, she loved him as she had loved him on the day of their wedding. She wanted to be comforted by him and never leave his side. With these thoughts came the same giddy love from twenty years ago. She yearned with her whole being that she had not given in to love early but had waited until she was married and had Preston's child. It was a fantasy—a thought she had wished for so very many times in had carved grooves in her mind. She had often dreamed of bearing Preston's child to comfort herself. Then she hated herself for not wishing she had kept her illegitimate baby. She felt afraid of the moon—the spotlight exposing the criminal.

The refreshing cool of the ocean breeze changed into an uncomfortable chill, prompting her to go inside. Confession. Maybe she would confess to Preston. Tanya slid open the door and played with the idea. What if she told him after all these years? *Preston, I had my unborn baby murdered when I was sixteen, before I married you.* She imagined his disappointed expression, a head lowered in shame. He would regret that he had married her. He would be sad every time he saw her face. When his eyes landed on her, he would say, "Oh, hello, my darling," in a low, humiliated voice. No, she could never tell him. It was as impossible as erasing the past.

The stateroom was filled with a chilling darkness. Tanya rubbed her arms, wishing she had packed a warmer nightgown. The sound of Preston's dim breathing could barely be heard above the steady rumble of the engine. Tanya exhaled heavily as she crawled into bed. She was tired but could never sleep well. She had love, respect, and family but could never truly receive these gifts. She felt like a fraud, a bad woman who was play acting as an affectionate wife and mother.

Suddenly, the Cardinal's offer was quite appealing. Tanya wanted to go to confession.

Connor Alekseev brought two glasses of French rosé wine on a tray sprinkled with crimson rose petals to the veranda of the master suite, where Orlean Cavenaugh and Ronald Jennings lounged intimately in a loveseat. "Can I bring you anything else?" he offered.

"No. Nothing else," said Ronald sharply.

Connor slipped away.

Ronald wrapped his flabby arms more tightly around Orlean. "Finally, it's just the two of us. Have I told you yet how extremely beautiful you are, my dear?"

"Yes, you have." Orlean laughed pleasantly. Ronald's flattery was like the taste of white chocolate mousse, far too creamy and sweet. But for some reason she gobbled it up. She gazed out at the vast ocean. Some black clouds hid the moon. The sea breeze played with the thin silk butterflies on the skirt of her dress. What luxury she possessed—a magnificent yacht charging through warm Atlantic waters, a goblet of expensive rosé in her hand, and a wealthy lover who showered her with pretty lies.

"What is the point of luxury? Does it really matter?" she whispered. It was all a show that she had applauded for far too often, but the play was ending soon; it would all be gone. But Ronald didn't know that.

"Of course it matters," Ronald protested. "Luxury distinguishes us from others."

"Are you sure it's not poison?" Orlean took another gulp of wine.

Two hands affectionately clutched her shoulders. "Are you all right, Orlean?" His voice attempted to be soft and kind.

Saying no just didn't seem to fit the occasion. "Oh yes, I'm perfectly all right." Orlean dropped a rose petal into her glass of wine and drowned the crimson flake.

7

The Past

Fourteen-year-old Connor leapt behind a hill of desert stones and golden barrel cactus, hiding from the enemy.

"Ah, you made it back safely." The team captain, Blake Stonewell, welcomed Connor with a pat on the back.

"Yes," Connor panted. "I didn't get hit."

"Good." Blake scooted up and peered over the hill. "They're coming. Get your boffer ready."

Boffers were swords fashioned from PVC pipes, pool noodles and duct tape—the weapons of backyard warfare. They caused a sharp, pulsing pain if you got hit.

"When we charge, I want you to run as fast as you can," Blake instructed. "It's your job to get the flag back here to home base." He smiled. "You're going to do great, Con. You're an excellent runner."

"Got it. And thank you!"

A youth who was all arms and legs approached from around the corner. Connor tensed for a second but then relaxed. "Phew! It's one of ours."

Blake greeted the new arrival, a fifteen-year-old by the name of Skander Greenwood.

"I'm glad you made it! We were just getting ready to charge for the flag." Blake chuckled, amused at himself. "I have to admit, I'm a bit nervous. Connor, your brother is pretty intimidating."

"You can't say that," Connor scolded. "You're our leader."

Blake shrugged. "All right, troops. Are you ready for the charge?"

"*Yes!*" Connor and Skander raised their boffer-swords high in the air.

"I think so, at least…" Skander added, gulping.

"We're just going to have to face our fears and do this," said Blake. "On the count of three. One. Two. Three!"

Scrambling over the rocky hill, the army of three charged for the flag. It was just a warped stick with a red T-shirt on it. But it was the flag, the goal, the sign of victory for the winning team.

Derek Alekseev, Connor's big brother and the leader of the opposition, was a blond and burly youth. He wielded his boffer with the utmost prowess. He was a true warrior with many victories under his belt. He also had two competent followers, Blake's little brother Diego Stonewell and Skander's little brother Gael Greenwood. And he was charging right at the same flag.

Connor sped ahead, dropping his boffer (per the rules) as he attempted to pry the flag out of the ground. "Guys! Cover me!"

Flanking his sides, Blake and Skander pressed into the enemy, exchanging hits and blocks with gray duct-tape swords.

Connor's heart ran a marathon as he finally removed the flag from the ground and sprinted back to base, but not without a pursuer in tow. Diego was right behind him.

"Get him!" Derek shouted, his voice deep and hoarse. "Get Connor!"

Connor's feet were like wings. The flag struggled in the wind, Connor's only inhibitor. He was almost at the base! But he could hear Diego's heavy breathing right behind him.

Whilst running, Diego Stonewell swung his sword, barely missing Connor's shirt.

Connor could still make it! He jumped with all his might and landed inside the circle of stones—which was home base.

"*Victory!*" Blake declared. "We have the victory!"

D uring supper, the boys and the girls ate separately. The boys gathered on the knee-high brick wall that surrounded the butterfly garden. The girls ate inside the gazebo, which was comfortably shaded by a lattice of intertwining green and purple wisteria vines. The moms and the small children socialized on the cushioned garden furniture, amongst the aromatic honeysuckle, rosemary, and lilac bushes.

Dressed in a rustling denim skirt and a long-sleeved shirt printed with bright pink flowers, Mrs. Alekseev approached the boys. "Would anyone like a piece of fresh bread?" she asked, passing by with a precious loaf of whole grain bread, baked with home-ground flour. Tangible wafts of steam rose from the thick slices.

"Definitely! Thank you, Mrs. Alekseev!" said Blake cheerily.

"Oh yes. Thank you, Mrs. Alekseev!" said Skander Greenwood.

"Thanks, Mom." Connor smiled as he placed the bread on top of his bowl of borscht.

Assured that the boys had plenty of food, Mrs. Alekseev returned to the moms.

As Connor chewed a spoonful of the hearty stew —made with deep red beets, chunks of lamb, cubed potatoes, and purple cabbage—he watched the girls in their long skirts. They were chatting rapidly about something. He was particularly interested in Joy Greenwood, a beautiful but strange girl with a long sheet of brown hair overlaid by two delicate braids that rejoined at the back. Connor had to get her attention somehow.

He had an idea.

Connor went around the back of the house and captured something. Then he walked up to the gazebo full of girls. They all stared at him.

"Hey Joy, I have something for you."

Joy squinted and blinked at the same time. "What's that?"

Connor opened his fist right on top of Joy's shoulder. A tan lizard dropped onto the fabric of her shirt.

"*Ahhhhhh!*" they all squealed, to Connor's delight.

Joy instantly brushed it off.

Terrified, the lizard scurried across the table, launched onto the gravel ground, and fled to the safety of the butterfly bushes.

Connor's older sister, Eliza Alekseev, scowled at him furiously, her white-blond braids flinging around. "We're having a wholesome, intellectual conversation, and you take it upon yourself to interrupt us with a lizard?" She made a sweeping motion with her hand. "Go away! Go back to your pitiful boyish small talk!"

Smirking, Connor turned to leave.

"Wait," said Joy Greenwood, holding up her plastic cup of water.

"Yes?" Connor responded hopefully.

"I have something for you too." Joy raised her cup and hurled the contents all over Connor's face and shirt. The girls roared with glee.

Shocked, embarrassed, and drenched in ice water, Connor wobbled back to the boys.

"Ha! Joy got you good," said Blake, holding a stomach full of laughter and borscht.

After dinner, everyone gathered out front beside hefty SUVs that were made for transporting large families. Mrs. Greenwood and Mrs. Stonewell were expressing their gratitude to Mrs. Alekseev with warm hugs and whispers about homeschool curriculums. The girls were huddled together, their long skirts blocking any intruding boys. And the boys were leaning against the Greenwoods' blue SUV.

Blake shook Derek's hand. "I'll see you when you get back."

"It's going to be a while," Derek responded.

"I'll see you at JROTC on Thursday," Connor interjected.

"Yes. Be ready for some marching, Parrot," said Blake.

Derek chuckled. "Careful. If you call him Parrot he might copy you forever."

"No, he won't." Suddenly Blake put Connor into a head lock and rubbed his knuckles into his skull. "He just liked my speech at co-op."

After a brief tussle, Connor broke free, smiling vividly. "Your speech may or may not have had something to do with it. You guys are like cousins now. I've got to be a part of things."

"I'll see you there, Parrot." Blake shook his hand, firmly but kindly.

Mrs. Stonewell said farewell to every single person there, besides her own children of course. When she got to Connor, she appraised him with such powerful motherly affection it was hard to look at. "Connor Alekseev, I have a word for you— something I believe I was meant to tell you."

Connor's interest was piqued. "Okay. Please tell me."

Mrs. Stonewell smiled and revealed the phrase. "The push and pull of friendship will be important throughout your life. In this way, you will learn how to become the man you are meant to be."

Connor was dumbfounded. "Oh my gosh! My dad said something like that to me just this morning! What a crazy coincidence."

"Coincidences do not exist." Mrs. Stonewell gave him a hug. "We'll see you later!"

The Alekseevs waved as the two SUVs drove off down the dusty road, the rocky-faced mountains looming in the distance.

Derek smacked Connor on the shoulder. "I'm going inside. Good game today."

Connor lingered in the front yard, watching the Stonewells' gray SUV turn down at the end of the street. He had really enjoyed being on Blake's team for capture the flag. Connor was not accustomed to having friends who were much older than himself. His friends were usually around his age or a year younger. But Blake Stonewell was two years older. He was mature and tall and working a job, one of Derek's buddies. Connor and Derek usually had separate friends. But this time Connor was actually becoming friends with Blake. He was like a new big brother.

He also wondered about the phrase from Mrs. Stonewell. It was as though he had caught a glimpse of his future through the lens of a telescope. It flashed and flickered and quickly disappeared. But Connor felt unique and more alive, yet disoriented at the same time. Going forward with this unusual motivation, Connor was sure his life would change for the better.

8

Connor tried to sleep on his top bunk while the chef snored obnoxiously below. He turned on his stomach, resting his head on his forearm, and peeked out the porthole. The dark water reflected silver light while the restless waves swam up and down, playing with the reflections. Connor glided his thumbnail along the grain of the stained-wood bunk railing. He was surprised by the recollection. He hadn't thought of those precious family gatherings in years. And he didn't want to think about them now. Those days were long gone.

With a heavy sigh, Connor surrendered to wakefulness. He climbed out of the bunk, dressed warmly enough, and wandered out into the yacht. His cabin was on the very bottom of the vessel, the same level as the library. He resolved to find a book and read for a while. Maybe that would help him to relax.

But there was already a soft glow of lamplight ahead. Was someone else awake? Once Connor passed the engine room and the cinema, he saw a young woman browsing the floor-to-ceiling bookshelves. It was Shanlee Jennings.

"Looks like we had the same idea," said Connor.

Two books toppled out of Shanlee's hands, landing on the floor with a loud crash. "Oh no!" She covered her mouth with her hands, as if it would help to stop the noise that had already ended. "You startled me." She stooped down. "Oh, these poor books. Look, the binding on one of them is cracked."

Connor rushed over to assist her. "I'm sorry. I didn't mean to scare you. People say I have quiet footsteps."

"That's okay." She cradled the wounded books. "I hate to think what Lady Cavenaugh will say, though."

"Don't worry about her," said Connor. "She hardly ever comes down here. And I've never seen her read. I don't think she'll care. But we can set the books aside if you want to ask her about it tomorrow."

"Hmmm…" Shanlee tapped her lips with her forefinger. "I think that's a splendid idea. Let's do that."

"What books are they, anyways?"

"Sit down with me and I'll show you."

The light from the pool above cast dancing watery lines all over the library. They stepped across the transparent floor to a sprawling leather couch with abundant pillows.

"This place smells like someone was smoking a cigar," Connor commented as he clicked on a lamp.

"Yes, it has such an old money feeling to it, very different from the rest of the yacht." Shanlee took a few steadying breaths on the couch.

"It has a few modern touches. Let me show you." Connor sprang up, reaching for a light switch that was hidden between two bookshelves. The floor illuminated into a deep sapphire glow. Shanlee's face lit up with delight as she stared at the rushing water below the transparent glass floor. "Oh my goodness!"

Connor smiled. It was good to see her cheer up after the book spill. And she was quite pretty. The extra light brought out her elegant features—her soft complexion, her mesmerizing eyelashes, and her high cheekbones. All Connor wanted to do was sink into the burgundy leather couch and continue gazing at her face—and maybe get to know her a bit.

"It's *Little Women* and *A Tale of Two Cities*," said Shanlee.

"You've picked one of my favorites," said Connor. "I'm a Dickens fan."

"Oh really?" Shanlee replied excitedly. "What do you like so much about Dickens?"

Each on opposite sides of the vast couch, Connor and Shanlee talked for hours, keeping their voices low so as not to rouse anyone else on board. They played a game of two truths and a lie, wherein Connor discovered that Shanlee had never been out of the country before, she favored bloodhound dogs, and she wanted to be a lawyer like her father. Connor revealed his interest in visiting every single country in Europe, his belief that a well-trained Great Dane was the absolute best form of pet, and his aspirations to work for law enforcement one day. Soon, an old grandfather clock chimed for the second time.

"Is it really two a.m.?" Shanlee remarked.

Connor yawned. "Huh. It is. Crazy. I guess we'd better go back to our cabins."

They meandered down the hallway, whispering as quietly as possible. The doorway to her cabin was like the threshold to her home, and Connor was walking her back like a hometown boy. "Can I give you a hug goodnight?" he asked.

"Yes, for sure. Definitely."

"Definitely? I like the sound of that." They shared a wonderful, long embrace. And something happened. They didn't want to separate. But eventually they did, saying, "I'll see you tomorrow," far too many times.

Above all the resting passengers in the captain's bridge on deck four of the *Chrysalis*, Captain Thomas Neals held the wheel of the yacht while he waited for his chief officer. The silence was welcome to the captain, allowing him to think. The light glow of his instruments and the tranquil night wind were a solace unmatched. However, his aged features and his carefully trimmed gray mustache did not show peace or pleasure about his solace. Instead, they showed humorless introspection. When he was alone and the night was old, the deepest of thoughts came to him. *What am I living for? Who am I helping?* He served his employer, Lady Cavenaugh, and instructed his chief officer, Brock Minton. He ate and he slept…was that all of his life? The country he once knew was falling apart; people weren't thinking about what they did or cared whether they did it with honor. People had forgotten honor. Had he ever met a young man or young woman who truly honored others? Did anyone in this new generation respect the sacrifice of fallen soldiers?

Thomas Neals thought back to the Vietnam War. He recalled what his brother had said. "You have talent, Thomas. Come and serve your country."

Thomas had replied foolishly, "I don't believe in this war. It is against the American Constitution. I cannot fight a war that is against the American Constitution."

But when the letter came saying, "…he died for his country," Thomas wished he had gone to war with his brother. He later found out that his brother died in a Vietnamese torture room while they tried to pry secrets from him. In those youthful days of his, two years after he had received the letter, Thomas joined the navy, but by that time the war had ended.

If only he could tell others the torment of living a life as a coward. A man can reason himself out of anything, even honoring the dead—even love. But no matter how he tried to explain the wrong in cowardice, in reasoning yourself out of doing what's right, no one listened; they only replied with their opinions about the Vietnam War and how wrong it was. They didn't get it. No one seemed to understand how it wasn't about the political motive or the ethical opinion; it was about honor, respect, integrity, and love. Love is not lust, and love is not kissing and caressing; love is discipline, loyalty, and self-sacrifice.

Brock Minton climbed the stairs behind the captain, who turned to hand over the wheel. "Just keep the course steady," Thomas began in his low voice. "It's a beautiful night. You'll enjoy it." Eager to take on the exciting responsibility, Brock stepped up and grasped the wheel.

"Okay," Brock replied. "I'll keep a steady course."

Brock had dark hair sharply buzzed in military style. His face was strong with solid cheekbones, and his expressions were full of the thrill of adventure.

"Yes. Goodnight, son." Thomas Neals turned and headed down to his room.

After journeying through the maze of stairs and narrow hallways he arrived at his stateroom and clicked on the reading lamp. The shadows were thicker tonight.

Thomas decided he had done all he could in this life. He had trained Brock as best he could. He had served a few years in the Navy. What would happen if he died? His wife had passed away without bearing children; few people were at her funeral. And what was he doing now? Enabling a rich old lady who had little regard for right and wrong. If his brother were there, he would be saddened to discover how Thomas was spending the twilight years of his life. He was a great captain who did the bidding of a rich widow, for more money than he had a right to own, and spent his free time alone in his house in Maine. Why did he keep going on like this? It was a lonely life.

He reached for the small glass of water by his bed and the liquid slid down his throat, scraping and hurting. An icy gust raced through the room, clawing at his skin. *Why is the room so cold?* he wondered. *I thought it was a warm night.* He didn't want to think anymore and clicked off the light.

9

The morning light fell into Orlean Cavenaugh's bedroom as she woke to the sound of knocking. Careful not to wake the man sleeping beside her, Orlean put on her robe and walked to the door. "Yes, Najah? What is it? Why are you breathing so fast?"

"Ma'am." The maid glared through terrified eyes. "The captain is dead."

The boat rocked, resting silently with anchors set, while twelve people looked down at the body in the captain's cabin. It was in the bed with eyes closed; a knife was in the body's left pectoral with the right hand clutching it. All waited in silence while the new arrivals, Lady Cavenaugh and Ronald Jennings, observed.

"These were left on the nightstand," Preston Jennings informed Lady Cavenaugh, breaking the silence as he pointed at a blue origami butterfly, blotched with ink, and a page of white paper with handwriting on it.

"What is this? A paper butterfly and a poem?" she asked.

Preston nodded. "Shall I read it?"

"Yes, do so." Orlean's eyes glazed over as she stood motionless.

They all listened as Preston abided:

> "Spear the soul,
> wring the heart;
> my hands are folded,
> your lives depart.
>
> "The old Deep Blue,
> his wings curled and cracked.
> Free, free you,
> eleven months leak the black.
>
> "Sin, the blessed touch,
> revere the pleasing shimmer.
> Flames are not too much,
> soon sip the scarlet dinner.
>
> "Molding won't set this mind free,
> I must intervene.
> Wretched captain, don't hate me,
> I'm just a loving team.
> —The Glass Shadow"

"Oh, how sad." Orlean sighed with her head low. "He killed himself."

"Are you sure about that?" Preston stared at the body suspiciously.

Orlean gasped. "Yes. I think it's rather obvious. Are you suggesting he was *murdered*?"

"I'm only considering the possibility."

"I don't think wild ideas are at all appropriate at this time," Orlean responded indignantly. "Would you mind keeping your thoughts to yourself?"

"Of course, Lady Cavenaugh. I apologize for being so inconsiderate." Preston gave her a bow of respect.

Orlean shook her head. "I suppose that means he wanted us to continue and not worry about him."

Ronald glanced at her questioningly while all the others waited for her to explain.

"When he said, 'free, free you,' he was telling us that we are free to go on and shouldn't worry about him." She felt heartless about pointing that out instead of respecting him.

"That is rather dramatic, don't you think?" Preston remarked.

"Can you blame him?" Orlean replied. "Can you blame him for leaving this life in a beautiful way, for writing a poem that expressed what he thought of his existence? He had every right to take his life in the way he wanted, to die in fading style—in art. How can we look down on him for ending his life when it seemed to him empty and void? He must have thought that he had lived long enough. Now he is where he wanted to be, in peace." No one else spoke, for the moment demanded silence. Orlean didn't want to stand there any longer. "We should leave his room now. Brock?"

"Yes?" he answered.

"Continue the course toward Europe. Xenon?" She turned to the chef.

"Yes, ma'am?"

"Finish making breakfast and serve our guests. I'm going to my room. Have Connor serve mine to me in bed." With a slight hesitation, she took the poem and origami butterfly from the nightstand. They all looked at her. "Why are you all staring at me? Go on! Do whatever you were doing before! Go! Leave this room."

They did as she said.

The old Deep Blue, his wings curled and cracked. Free, free you, eleven months leak the black…

Orlean sat alone in her bed behind the light-blue mosquito net draped around her as she read the handwritten poem again. She had opened all her windows, inviting the wind to enter. The morning light had gone and was now replaced with an overcast, darkening sky. The mosquito net flapped in the breeze with the ugly lady inside. She was ugly, and she knew it. She had dyed her hair to make herself appear younger, but her face was wrinkled and blemished out of her control. The dark spots had spread all over her body.

Her captain had left her. If only she could have told him how much she had appreciated and respected him; she still did. But now he had left her. Her friend was gone.

She felt starved and parched like a lone, wandering creature of the savanna. But water and food couldn't cure this yearning. Now her world was getting more alone. The coming storm would sweep through and take all that she loved—whatever was left that she had to hold on to. The flies that nibbled and sucked her blood, creatures only there for themselves, her only company, were leaving her. What would happen when they got to Europe? Would she find other pests to take more from her— worse than the ones before? They would appear to love her but in truth they all hated her; no one loved her. She was in a void world where her only friends were those that got something from her.

She heard a knock. It was probably Connor with her breakfast. She wasn't hungry. She couldn't eat even if she wanted to. This was too upsetting. "Come in." She tried to be loud.

"Orlean?" It was her brother.

She got out of bed, walked across the tile floor, and went to greet him. "Hello, Sabino." She attempted to smile. It was strange talking to her brother after so many years. She felt like she didn't know how to say things anymore. "Come, sit down." They went out to the lounge on the veranda.

"I'm sorry, Orlean. This must be deeply troubling." His eyes were solemn and compassionate.

Orlean shook and shook her head, her lips pressing hard against each other. "You have no idea!" Her voice broke and she began to cry. He picked up a tissue box from the coffee table and put it beside her. She kept shaking her head. "He was the last person who was truly honorable that I had around me. He was selfless. He was kind, maybe blunt at times, but a good man. How can you replace a lost life? It's wrong. It's...it's terrible."

"I'm here for you, sister," Sabino began. "I know that we haven't talked for over forty years, but I love you as my sister. But more importantly, God loves you, and he wants you to know him and find the joy, the purpose, and the everlasting life he has for you."

"God?" She sniffled. "Why did you have to bring up *God?* What has God ever done for me? Besides, what have *I* ever done for God?"

"He is willing to forgive your offenses."

"How do you know there even is a God? Whatever it is, there could be more than one. Neptune might exist! You limit yourself to one God when there might be many who are lording their superiority over us. Whatever they are, I know that they hate me. And I hate them because they hate me."

The cardinal was somber for a minute. "I'm grieved to hear this. You might not believe me but God is a very loving person."

"I don't believe you."

"He sent his only Son to die for us, sacrificing part of himself in the process. He gave himself to us and took away our sins once and for all—"

"Stop babbling about God!" Orlean exhaled in a frustrated tone and snatched a tissue while she rubbed her right eye. "Don't try to persuade me to join your value system. I don't believe it and I never will." She blew her nose loudly and Sabino left her. She held her head high with pride, for she had persuaded herself that she was right to hate the gods.

10

Connor stood in the bar on deck two, polishing the freshly cleaned glasses from lunch. He looked past the pool and the hot tub. The morose sky hid the sun and cast pale shadows, causing time to feel cruel. The boat rocked as it barreled across the water, rattling the wine goblets. It would probably rain soon.

The little boy, Clayton Jennings, approached the sandy stone pillar beside the bar. It was decorated with relief carvings of stingrays leading a school of tiny fish.

"It's a beautiful pillar, huh?" said Connor.

"What?" Clayton replied.

"You've been staring at that carving for a while now. Is it cool?" Connor smiled casually.

"Yeah, I guess. I was just think'n about stuff."

"Can I get you something? How about a Coke?"

"Sure. That sounds great." Clay walked over and sat on one of the barstools, his curious face just tall enough to rise above the counter. Connor opened the can and poured the beverage into a glass with some ice.

"Here's your order, boss," said Connor playfully, setting the glass in front of him. "Your name is Clayton, right?"

"Yes." He took a sip and set down his glass. "But I like to be called Clay. That's my weel name."

"Okay then, I'll call you Clay. How old are you?"

"Seven," said Clay confidently. "How old are you?"

"I'm twenty-three," Connor replied.

Clay took another sip. "Do you play any sports?"

"I was a blue belt in karate in high school," said Connor. "I also like to run, but just for fun."

"Are you a fast wunner?"

Connor shrugged but decided to play it up. "I'm so fast. I bet I could even outrun you," he said teasingly. "If we were on land I would race you. Do you think you would beat me?"

Clay brightened. "I don't know. You are much taller than me." He craned around, spending a few seconds surveying the pool. "Wanna wace me to the hot tub?"

"Sorry, I can't." Connor picked up another glass to polish. "I don't think Lady Cavenaugh would like it. But, when we get to Europe, I will race you. Okay?"

"Okay. You're on!" Beaming, Clayton slipped off the barstool and bolted across the room, where his older sister had just appeared. "Shanlee!" Overly exuberant, Clayton charged into her knees.

"Oof!" Shanlee sidestepped him, as if she had done this many times before, and picked him up. "I think you're getting too big for this." She set him down. "You are much heavier than you used to be." She giggled, catching Connor's stare.

Connor graciously gestured toward the barstools. "Can I get you anything, Miss Jennings?"

Shanlee strolled up, wearing a white summer dress that was decorated with purple irises. "Oh, so you're a bartender too?" Taking her place on a stool, she rested her chin delicately on her hand. "Steward, bartender, and swing dance instructor. My, my, don't you have a diverse array of talents. Anything else on your resumé?"

Connor chuckled, appreciating the levity. "Oh, just a few other things." He smirked.

Shanlee suddenly turned serious. "So, how are you doing, after what happened with the captain?"

"Oh, I'm fine. I didn't know him well. But I know that Brock is an excellent chief officer. He will safely guide us to Europe."

Shanlee leaned in and whispered, "Do you really think it was suicide?"

"I don't know," Connor answered. "I only started working here a week ago."

Tanya Jennings entered the bar, her expression grave. She addressed them both. "Excuse me, my husband is calling a meeting upstairs. It's very important. Please, join us now."

Serious as two soldiers holding a coffin, Preston Jennings stood with Brock Minton, their backs to the window, as they waited for the ten other people to settle into the lounge by the dining table on deck three. Tanya Jennings glanced uneasily at the others, the frightened and wide-eyed Najah Hasan poised on the sofa beside her. Cardinal Sabino Verdone scrutinized the painting above the fireplace in the middle of the room. Durand blinked many times from behind his thick glasses, asking, "What's up?" but no one answered him. Ronald Jennings was positioned across from Preston with his brow furrowed, glaring at his brother and trying to ascertain what he knew. The chef was next to Ronald, showing the signs of deepest boredom.

"Well?" Orlean prompted impatiently, still agitated by the tragedy of the morning.

After Clayton, Shanlee, and Connor pulled up a few of the dining table chairs to sit on, Preston began. "I have received some disturbing news. Our acting captain, Brock Minton, has just informed me that the radio communications have been tampered with and are no longer operable."

A few people gasped at this.

"I have also discovered that my international cell phone is missing. It was equipped with a built-in remote satellite so that I could make calls from the middle of the sea. I believe you will find that your cell phones, if international, are missing as well."

Orlean gasped. "Are you saying we have no communication with the rest of the world?"

"What?" Ronald jumped to his feet.

"Yes, I am," Preston responded.

Ronald plopped back on the sofa, shaken by the news.

"Who would do that?" Tanya asked, still digesting the severity of her husband's words.

"This leads me to only one conclusion. There is a murderer in our midst."

"Are you still pushing that idea?" Orlean shook her head. "The captain must have done all that last night."

"I might have considered that, Lady Cavenaugh, if it weren't for this." He held up a brown origami caterpillar. "If you remember, last night at dinner, there was a paper caterpillar identical to this one, but blue, and it was left on the table. It was the same blue of the paper butterfly found beside the deceased captain this morning. This brown caterpillar was on the table at breakfast. I believe it is a death threat."

Everyone fell silent, waiting for Preston to continue.

"I have toured the yacht with Mr. Minton today by Lady Cavenaugh's permission, and we have determined that there is no one else besides us on this vessel. As such, the murderer must be someone in this room."

Several members of the group shot uneasy glances at each other but quickly looked back at Preston. Orlean, however, kept her gaze fixed on the lawyer. "I don't believe it," she declared in a chilling voice. "You are making this up."

Preston analyzed her expression for a moment. "I am only trying to do what I can to help save our lives."

Orlean laughed, a derisive *hmmm* laugh. "So, you think another one of us is going to be murdered?"

"Yes."

"Well, you're wrong. It's not true." She stood and turned to walk out. "I am going to my room. Xenon?"

"Yes?" the chef replied irritably as if Preston's words were only a stupid joke.

"Have dinner served on the table by the pool. I will be in my room. Brock, don't you dare stop our course!" She strode past the wine cellar and slammed the door to the master suite at the end of the hallway. The chef got up and went to the kitchen.

"That is unfortunate," Preston said as he reached for a clipboard with paper on it. He handed the clipboard to Connor. "I would like all of us who remain here to write a phrase on this piece of paper, so that I can compare the handwriting with the handwriting on the poem. I will have to obtain the handwriting of Lady Cavenaugh and Mr. Leveque at a later time."

Connor clicked the pen. "What phrase should I write?"

Preston shrugged. "It can be anything. I put down the phrase 'I just visited New York City' at the top."

"Okay." Connor copied the phrase and then passed the clipboard to Shanlee. The writing set made its rounds through the group. Clayton took his time scratching out a phrase, and Shanlee nudged him to pass it on. The cardinal gravely accepted the clipboard with two hands, as if he were signing a coup d'état agreement. Durand blinked several times. Ronald's entire face reddened in offense as he wrote some kind of phrase on the page. Najah chewed on the pen for a minute, but suddenly scribbled on it when the others stared at her. After writing her part, Tanya looked to her husband helplessly as she handed him the clipboard.

"What would you like me to do?" Sabino Verdone asked Preston in his most serious voice.

"The only sensible thing that any of us can do is to stay in the same room so we can see each other. That gives us our best chance for catching the murderer. But Lady Cavenaugh is being very foolish. There isn't much we can do for her now."

The cardinal nodded in agreement.

"Do we just *sit* here?" Tanya asked, still in disbelief.

"Yes, you, and all of my children, should stay in this room with the cardinal. We must get to the mainland as soon as we can. My brother and I, if he will abide"—he glanced at Ronald—"will go with Mr. Minton to the bridge deck. We must have three or more persons in a room at a time. Mr. Alekseev and Ms. Hasan," he addressed Connor and Najah. "For the safety of your employer, could you try to accompany Lady Cavenaugh? If she doesn't allow you into her room, then there is nothing more we can do. Come right back here if she denies you entrance." He gestured to the sofas and the armchairs. "This lounge will be our meeting spot for dinner."

Najah shot a fearful look at Connor and turned toward the master suite. Not knowing what else to do, Connor followed.

11

A sheet of darkness smothered the *Chrysalis* in cryptic shadows as the yacht tried to race like a snail crossing miles. It was but a speck in the vast ocean. Water darted down in tiny beads, ringing in the ears of everyone on board. Brock Minton did not join the eleven others for dinner; he was busy keeping their course straight.

The meal was served inside. Even though Lady Cavenaugh's orders were usually obeyed, she couldn't boss around the storm. Najah and Connor were glad to dine with the others. However, the chef didn't feel very honored to dine with them; he would have preferred the pleasure of his own company. Few said words while they ate. Few could think of words.

Lady Cavenaugh disliked the lack of conversation. "It really is ridiculous." The glass and silver clicking ended as all listened to her. "None of us is a murderer." Her wry grin wasn't very comforting. "The captain had his say. Maybe he didn't want us to make any fuss about his death and made sure of that by silencing our communications. He knew about the sea. He must have thought that we didn't need to communicate with the outside world."

"How do you explain the brown paper caterpillar?" Preston retorted skeptically.

"One of us must have seen the paper bug the captain put on the table last night and tried to make a duplicate out of some brown paper lying around. Art does that to you. The captain is trying to tell us that he is free, that he is released. He is happy now, and we should be happy for him. Panicking is probably the last thing he wanted us to do. Besides, I asked Brock about the eleven ink spots on the blue butterfly. He said that the captain's only brother spent eleven months in the service and died in Vietnam. I myself have heard him talking about his brother and their childhood a number of times. This must have brought him down. Maybe he felt responsible for his brother's death and the guilt was too much for him. Guilt *is* hard to deal with." She took a sip of her wine. Her words reminded her of the things that caused guilt in her own past. Shreds of unhappy memories came to her like an acquaintance from long ago.

The chef allowed a light smile of amusement to slip onto his features. Orlean did not like this reaction. Everyone else just pointed their noses at the mahogany table.

Orlean was displeased when Sabino, Preston, and Tanya blatantly rebuffed the dessert. She and the little boy were the only ones who ended up consuming the tantalizing mango cream puffs with lemon-tangerine glaze. The rain poured outside the window as she watched Clayton slurp the filling out of the golden brown shells. Orlean preferred adult company during dessert.

R aindrops are liquid pebbles—pebbles that pound, pebbles that knock, reminders. They continue pounding, regardless of your attempts to stop them. You might go into a house, in a nice, cozy room, and turn on lights, but the rain can still be heard on the roof, windows, and skylights…like guilt. Connor wondered if little Clay felt guilty about something, for he winced with sadness while they played cards in the lounge on deck three.

"Connor?"

"Yeah?"

"Can I tell you something?"

"Sure, of course."

"It's not a good thing." Clay hid most of his face behind his fan of cards.

"I won't hold it against you."

This brought some relief to Clay, who set down his cards. He glanced over his shoulder to make sure his family was out of earshot. Tanya, Preston, Shanlee, and Durand were speaking in low tones across the room. Seemingly convinced that they were far enough away, Clay faced Connor again. He took a deep breath and whispered, "A couple months ago,

I lied to my mommy about being sick when I actually wasn't. For two days, I pretended to be too sick to get out of bed."

Connor restrained himself from smiling. "Well, thank you for telling me. But can I tell you something too?"

"Yeah?" Clay whispered.

"I did the same thing when I was around your age."

Clay's jaw dropped. "What? You did? Why?"

"To get out of doing schoolwork as well."

"Did you ever tell your mommy?"

"No, but I wished that I did." Connor gestured toward Mr. and Mrs. Jennings. "I won't tell them. But do you think you should?"

Clayton lowered his head apprehensively. "They might put me on westriction."

Connor chuckled this time. "I think they have a few more serious things on their minds right now. It's probably a good time, actually."

"Okay. I'll tell Mommy." Without another word, Clay scrambled over to the lounge chairs and pulled on Tanya's shirt.

Tanya was controlling her expressions as her son finished, listening attentively like a good mother would. *Look at this brave boy,* she thought. *He's telling me the thing he is most afraid to share and he's doing just fine.*

Tanya felt inspired, emboldened. Maybe she could do the same thing. She would have to find the cardinal.

Clayton stopped talking, his head sinking into his body as he fearfully awaited his mother's response.

"You know what, sweetie?" she said.

"What?"

"I still love you." Tanya stretched out her arms. "Can I have a hug?"

Clayton jumped into her arms, pulling her down a little. "I love you too, Mommy!"

"Why don't you go back with your father," Tanya instructed. "I need to do something."

Tanya slipped away from the group in the deck three lounge, winding down the stairwell below the crystal chandelier. Deep walnut panels surrounded her, exhibiting the flowing grains of the wood. When she reached the eggshell-colored hallway where five staterooms were located on deck two, she halted at the doors. *This is mine and Preston's room; I know that's the captain's room because of this morning.* Tanya shuddered. *But which one is the cardinal's?* Cardinal Sabino Verdone had retired to bed about an hour earlier. She suspected that he must still be awake. It might be worth knocking on the three other doors. On the other hand, she didn't want to be rude.

A thud sounded from behind her.

Tanya gasped, whirling around. The sliding glass doors to the outdoor pool remained closed. Suddenly forfeiting her search, Tanya scrambled up the stairwell, back to the dining room and lounge on deck three.

12

The Past

Fourteen-year-old Connor Alekseev charged down the weather-worn track, flailing to the finish line in third place. He wore a military-green T-shirt and black shorts, just like all the other boys. Connor leaned over to catch his breath, pressing his palms on his knees, as he stood above a prairie dog hole. A golden sunset enveloped the Las Vegas skyline behind him.

"Well done, Con." Another fourteen-year-old boy slapped Connor on the back. "You were fast."

"Thanks, Logan," Connor muttered between strained inhales. "I wasn't the fastest, though."

"You were faster than me," said Logan, a freckled youth with a buzzcut. "One of these days I'm going to work out between these weekly JROTC meetings so I can get better. That's what you do, right?"

"I run two miles almost every day." Connor watched a tall and skinny seventeen-year-old boy clasp hands with his buddy. "Hey, don't you think Blake Stonewell is pretty cool?"

"Yeah, I guess. He's good-looking. But he doesn't really stand for anything."

"I disagree," said Connor. "Blake is compassionate. He's good to people. Like, if someone had a dark secret that they never told anyone before, they could tell it to Blake. I want to be like him. Don't you?"

Logan shrugged. "I'd rather be like one of my older brothers."

Even though his friend disagreed with the idea, Connor started planning how he would tell Blake his dark secret.

About a week later, while his siblings did their schoolwork, Connor finished typing an email to Blake Stonewell.

Dear Blake,

I wanted to tell you something that I've never told anyone else before. You seem really trustworthy, so I'm just going to go ahead and say it. I just ask that you please keep it to yourself. For about a year now, I've had a problem of looking at inappropriate pictures on the internet. I've even had thoughts about kissing you. It's weird to talk about, and I'm not entirely sure what to do. But I just wanted to come clean about this. I'm trying to change and get better.

I understand if you don't want to be my friend anymore.
Sincerely,
Connor

His finger hovered over the mouse for a moment. And then he pressed *send*.

Connor was nervous at the next JROTC meeting. Then, Blake walked up, clapped his hand on Connor's shoulder, and said, "How are you doing, my friend?"

Connor was overcome with relief. To be known and loved is happiness.

"Thank you so much for accepting me, Blake," said Connor, trying to express his immense gratitude.

"Of course I accept you, man!" said Blake. "Everybody has problems. But I think you should tell your parents about it."

"Hmm, I don't know." Connor scuffed his shoe on the floor. "Telling you was hard enough."

"You won't regret it. They'll help you."

"All right," Connor relented. "You give good advice. I'll tell my parents."

Blake grinned. "It's the right decision, Con. I know it. Can I tell my parents too?"

Connor considered the request for a moment. "I mean, your mom might be understanding. But I don't really know your dad."

"My parents are my closest friends," said Blake. "They're very wise. They can help too."

Connor shrugged. "Okay. Sure. Why not?"

A few days later, Connor walked up to the dining room table, where his parents sat. His dad had a white piece of paper in his hands.

Connor took his place at the other side. "You wanted to see me?"

Mr. Alekseev's face was scrunched up with a conundrum. "Mr. Stonewell just sent us this email. They are upset about the news that you have been looking at inappropriate photos online. They said you can talk with Blake in group settings, like at JROTC or other places, but you cannot hang out with him individually."

Connor frowned. "Wait, so I can't go running with him or anything?"

"Not individually."

"Right now, that is," Mrs. Alekseev added.

"Yes." Mr. Alekseev scanned down the email. "If you stop viewing inappropriate photos on the internet and having thoughts about kissing him, then over time, after trust is rebuilt, you can hang out with Blake one-on-one again."

13

Connor lay in his bed. The night was late and dark, as many a night before this, with no moonlight to leak in and remind him of life. The pattering of rain nearly drowned the snores of the chef but not completely. Connor remained awake. During these sleepless nights, his mind would often wander.

Why in the world did he keep recalling his high school years? Maybe it was because of the Jennings family. They reminded him of the homeschool community in which he had grown. There was warmth and kindness but problems too. Connor shook away the memories, trying to rid himself of the bittersweet conflation of feelings that came with them. Long nights can spin great webs of thought.

He sat up, dressed quietly, and slipped out to the hallway. Once again, there was a light ahead in the direction of the library. With his heart full of hope, Connor turned around the corner. The transparent glass floor was already illuminated by a sapphire glow. Behind the leather couch, a young woman with silky black hair was perusing through the shelves. "Did you find anymore Dickens novels?" he jibbed.

Shanlee's eyes widened in shock as she turned around. But then she smiled. "Nope. Do you have time to assist me in my search?"

"Yes, I'd like that." Connor stepped up beside her and began fiddling through the many books, grateful for the distraction.

B rock Minton stood alone in the captain's bridge, tightly clenching the wheel. The door behind him was locked as Preston Jennings had advised. "You can't trust anyone," he had said.

None of Lady Cavenaugh's words made any sense to Brock. Captain Neals would never have tampered with their communication instruments. He was a man of honor. Yes, maybe he didn't want them to be upset about his death, but was it even true that he had killed himself? Thomas Neals had been a solemn man, contemplative and serious, but would he thrust a knife into his heart? No, he wouldn't. Thomas Neals had respected life more than that. Brock remembered the captain telling him once, " 'Life, liberty, and the pursuit of happiness.' There was a reason why the Founding Fathers put life first." No, he would never have killed himself. The only other explanation was murder.

Murder. One of the eleven people sleeping below him was a murderer, but who? Who would have a reason to kill the captain? None of the guests seemed the type. The chef was a bad man, but he was too much of a lazy slob to do anything, wasn't he? What about Lady Cavenaugh? She had always thought favorably of the captain, but she had talked about his death so callously. She even ordered Brock to continue the course as if nothing had happened.

The possibility grew in Brock's mind, and he knew that he had to get the yacht back to America as soon as he could. He began turning the boat around. If only the communication equipment hadn't been sabotaged, then he would contact the authorities and ensure their rescue.

But wait!

He remembered the emergency two-way radio the captain had insisted on keeping. Of course! Why hadn't he thought of it before? Brock opened the cabinet behind him. There it was—the two-way radio. Now he could save his life and the lives of all the others on board who would have been killed! He might even be able to save the life of the killer's next intended victim. This would make him a hero.

Brock set the radio on the counter. He clicked the *on* button and tested the microphone. But it was night, a shrill, crawling night. *Would the murderer kill again, this very night?* he thought, a merciless ache in his chest. *Why are my eyes so dry?*

14

Orlean Cavenaugh stood with Preston Jennings under the morning sun outside the door of the bridge deck, showing him the smashed window. They didn't say a word. Ronald Jennings climbed up the stairs, gasping for breath as he joined them. They entered the captain's bridge, observing the body that was soaking in blood with a bullet hole in the upper back. The panel of instruments around the ship's wheel had been even more mutilated. It looked like someone had taken a knife and stabbed every button on the panel. Near Brock Minton's body was a stone-brown origami butterfly with an "x" splashed across the center in black ink. A white page with writing lay beside the butterfly. Orlean picked it up and handed it to Preston. He read to himself silently:

> Love the light dream,
> Clench the pretty mist.
> Drift, no longer seen,
> Valor made a jest.

Stand high in glory,
Gleam mind so far.
Now kiss the lowly,
Slime, slither, man, and law.

The Shadow plucked you from your stand,
Know I meant no harm.
Pillar, magic, sun-bathed land,
Gone, did you have charm?
—The Glass Shadow

The three exchanged glances soberly. There was no doubting that Preston Jennings had been right.

Chef Xenon Leveque sauntered over to the dining room table on deck three. Preston had called another meeting and nearly everyone was present. They were just waiting on the maid.

Orlean clicked her nails on the mahogany table, greatly agitated. "Connor, can you go find her? Now?"

Preston held up a hand. "No, Connor, please stay. I do not want anyone to depart."

"Excuse me!" Orlean burst out, causing Tanya and Shanlee to jump. "I am still the owner of this vessel! I give the orders here!"

Preston played it cool. "I'm sorry for speaking out of turn."

"If you won't let my steward do his job then just go on with it already!" Orlean demanded.

Preston took a deep breath, and as he did so, Najah Hasan shuffled into the room, wrapping her headscarf closely around herself. She wordlessly took a seat at the end of the table.

Orlean scowled at her. "Did you do it, Najah? After all this time you've worked for me? Did you kill my chief officer?"

Najah gulped. "No, ma'am. I did not."

Orlean pointed an accusatory finger at her maid. "I'm going to need more convincing than that!"

Preston reclaimed the reins of the conversation. "As Lady Cavenaugh has mentioned, Brock Minton was found dead this morning in the captain's bridge. All of the instruments have been tampered with. We have found no radio aboard this yacht. As of now, there is no one with the adequate knowledge and training to steer the yacht anywhere. We are currently adrift in the middle of the Atlantic Ocean."

"What's going to happen to us, then?" Ronald asked, his plump face turning a furious shade of crimson.

Preston sighed gravely. "We are about two days into the Atlantic Ocean. Hopefully, we have not drifted too far out of the shipping lanes. Our best chance now is to signal a passing ship. Thankfully, we have plenty of food and water on board…"

"Yeah, about that," said the chef with a startling menace in his voice.

All eyes turned to him.

The chef stood, sneering down at everyone.

"Xenon, what are you doing?" Orlean inquired, appalled.

The chef sent a threatening glower at his boss. "I'm surviving." He raised his voice. "Here's how it's going to go! I will lock myself in the kitchen, along with all of the food and drinking water."

Several people gasped. Ronald stood.

The chef removed a kitchen knife from inside his white coat pocket, bringing the group to silence. "If any one of you tries to enter the kitchen and get something to eat, I will kill you! Do you hear me? I do not care about *any* of your lives! All you are to me are singers of my praises! All you are to me are sources of income. But now, I've stowed away a ton of food and I don't care a speck about your lives! You can starve to death for all I care! Hear this and hear this well—until the murderer reveals themselves, or one of you catches them, all of the food and drink on this yacht belongs to me!"

The chef slowly backed toward the kitchen doors. When he passed out of sight, the noises of moving furniture and clicking metal sounded from the kitchen. The chef was preparing for a siege.

"Ah, poor Xenon," said Orlean, attempting to repair the shattered atmosphere. "I can tell he's taking Brock's death rather hard."

The sun peered past the few wisps of white fluff and down at Preston Jennings where he sat at the glass outdoor dining table on deck four. He was buried in thought with his chin resting on his clenched fist. Preston didn't clench his fists often but only for grave and serious occasions, as if he held something of great value between his fingers and palm—something he feared to lose but was slipping away.

Tanya Jennings shut the door tightly behind her in a fret as she hurried out to join him. "Preston, I-I think the chef is the murderer." She expected a response, but her husband seemed not to have heard.

Tanya lowered her head, taking the closest available chair. She knew she couldn't speak to her husband when he was in this state, for it meant that he was thinking of something of great importance. It had been this way for years. When she wanted to talk, needed to talk, Preston would be contemplating with that vexatious look. His face would take on the appearance of stone as if he were a statue lost deep in a dark and cold basement, concealed from the chaotic world above. When he was like this, Tanya would usually retreat and leave him to think no matter what issues were pressing and hold her burdens alone. She would think, *Why does he ignore me and treat me like this?* but would then be flushed with guilt, knowing that whatever he was thinking about had to be more important. "What a bad person I am" would always be her final words to herself. As she sat in the forlorn yacht upon the vast, unthinking ocean, she told herself the same familiar old words.

"I think I know who did it," Preston murmured finally.

"Yes, Preston? Who?"

He let out a sigh of utter pain and agony as if a piece of his soul had broken off. "Oh, how wicked! But how, how can I be sure? What horror! What hatred!"

"Preston, what are you saying?"

He turned to his wife and smiled weakly. "Hello, my dear. You are so lovely today. I'm sorry, but I must investigate more. It is of the greatest importance." With that, he left to go indoors.

Tanya sighed heavily. *I'll never be able to tell him.* Hopelessness crashed in on her as she gazed out at the open ocean. There was no other boat or land in sight.

And then she remembered Cardinal Sabino Verdone.

Connor, Shanlee, Clay, and Durand entered the quiet indoor dining room on deck three, venturing to find Mr. and Mrs. Jennings. They snuck past the kitchen, fearing the retribution of the chef. Through the small window, they spotted a stack of metal tables baring the door. They didn't dare utter a word. The only sound they heard was the soft, incessant rumble of the engine.

"Why aren't we moving?" Durand inquired, scrunching up his face behind his thick glasses. "If the engine's on, shouldn't the boat be moving?"

"I suppose it's keeping the electricity going," said Connor. "With the captain and Brock dead, no one is steering the boat. I think we're just floating here."

"In the middle of nowhere," Durand added.

Shanlee pressed her face with both hands. "I don't know where they are!"

"Maybe they're upstairs," Connor encouraged. "Would you like to go check?"

"Yes. Let's do that."

"I know! Why don't we split up and check different spots?" Clayton suggested perkily. He acted like they were playing a game of hide-and-go-seek.

As they turned toward the grand staircase, something on the dining table caught Shanlee's eye.

"Do you see that?" She ran to the table to investigate.

"What is it?" Connor followed.

Atop the polished wood, there was a bright-pink origami caterpillar, quietly introducing the now-certain threat.

15

Pink was just starting to show in the distant clouds. Tanya and the cardinal were alone on the very top of the yacht, called the sun deck, where there was only a small lounge and a covered hot tub. Tanya was taking deep, long breaths, forcing air into lungs that seemed hesitant to accept it.

"First we start by making the sign of the cross," said the cardinal.

Tanya did so, tapping her forehead, her chest, and her shoulders.

"Now, you say, 'Forgive me, Father, for I have sinned.' "

"Okay…okay." Tanya repeated the phrase. "Forgive me, Father, for I have sinned. I have never been to confession before." She looked to the cardinal. "Now what do I do?"

The elderly man gestured for her to continue. "Now, you say what is on your heart to confess."

"Okay…okay…" Tanya closed her eyes. "I was sixteen. I had gotten with a boy in high school. He was a senior." It was as if a lump of food was stuck in her throat. She swallowed and swallowed, but the lump wouldn't move. She had to continue anyway. "Then…then I got pregnant." Tanya gasped for air, hot tears rising into her eyes. "Look, I'm already crying."

"It's all right," said the cardinal. "Go on."

"Okay, I can do this." Tanya took another painful inhale. "I decided to seek out help. So, I drove to a clinic by myself. The staff were very nice. I was in a white room, talking with the nurse. She put her hand on my shoulder and she asked gently, 'Would you like it removed?' "

Tanya viciously shut her eyes. The lump grew larger; her nose was getting stuffy. And she cried. "And…and I said yes."

Tanya started to shake, slumping forward. "I'm sorry, I'm sorry. My baby! My baby!"

Cardinal Sabino Verdone was near tears himself. He could feel her burden, a secret that had grown heavier and heavier with each passing year. "Can I share a Scripture verse with you, Mrs. Jennings?"

Tanya was dabbing her eyes, blowing her nose, and gasping for breath. She could only manage a nod.

"It's from the New Testament, the book of First John, verses one and two. 'My little children, these things write I unto you, that ye sin not. And if any man sin, we have an advocate with the Father, Jesus Christ the righteous: And he is the propitiation for our sins: and not for ours only, but also for the sins of the whole world.' "

"What does propit…propitiation mean?" Tanya asked.

"It means atonement, the cleansing of sin," the cardinal answered. "Mrs. Jennings, I can tell that you are contrite, that you regret this and you never intend to do it again."

"That's just it, Mr. Verdone." Tanya revealed her swollen eyes. "There was a complication with the operation, an accidental incision in my uterus. I can never get pregnant again."

The cardinal closed his eyes, acknowledging the weight of this. "Oh, okay."

"But I do regret it." Tanya lowered her head. "I've regretted it for twenty-five years."

"I see that, and I believe God sees it too. Now, the next step is for me to instruct you with a penance appropriate for the sin." The cardinal thought for a moment. "You have suffered long enough, Tanya Jennings. I will not assign you an earthly penance. My only recommendation is that you receive the forgiveness of the Lord Jesus Christ." He made a cross motion over her. "God has brought about the ministry of reconciliation to the world through the death and resurrection of his Son. Your sins are atoned for. You are cleansed, Tanya Jennings. Go and sin no more."

Tanya inhaled a fresh breeze of salty Atlantic air, her cheeks wet with tears.

"Mommy?" said the voice of Clayton Jennings as he climbed up the exterior stairs that connected deck four to the sun deck. "There you are!" He ran up to his adopted mother. "Why are your eyes crying, Mommy? What's wrong? Why are your eyes crying?" he questioned, climbing up onto the teak wood bench and invading her space.

Tanya, however, was struggling to speak. "Clay, just sit down beside me for a minute, please."

The cardinal rose to his feet. "I will leave you two alone. Will you be all right, Mrs. Jennings?"

"Yes, yes, thank you," Tanya squeaked.

With that, the Cardinal bowed his head and made his way down the stairs.

"Mommy, do you need lots of hugs?" Clayton asked, wrapping his arms around her shoulders.

"Oh, thank you, sweetie. But can you please find me another tissue? There should be a pack in my purse."

Clayton dug through her blue leather bag. "Wow, do you have the whole living woom in here? Oh! Look what I found."

Tanya peered through her tears to find Clayton holding up a small middle-grade fiction book with an American flag on the cover. "It's your book! Would you like to read me a chapter?"

"Yes, of course I will." Clayton leaned snuggly against Tanya and began reading.

Tanya gazed out at the ocean. Pink brushstrokes floated upon the dark, floundering waves. Some waves drifted aimlessly, some arrogantly danced about, fustian as an unthinking prince in all his gaudy splendor. But as she stared, images from her high school years entered her mind, of the lockers in the hallways, of the old Ford that she used to drive, and of a small building tucked away behind a copse on the side of the road. She wondered why she didn't remember the boy from high school. She couldn't picture his face anymore.

" '...and Billy joined the Evolutionary War,' " Clayton was saying.

"Oh, it's Revolutionary War," Tanya corrected.

Clayton pulled the book so close to his face it nearly touched his eyelashes. "You're wight. Good weading, Mommy." And then he continued.

Tanya's mind drifted away. She wondered at what stage of pregnancy did a human spirit enter the fetus? Only God knew, she supposed. She wished she could speak with her baby. He or she would probably have been a beautiful child. Tanya was sure of it. She wondered at what age her child would be in heaven—a toddler or a full-grown adult? Another question to which only God knew the answer.

Tanya held her stomach, for it ached painfully. She focused on breathing—in and out, in and out. And then she heard the softest whisper, "I forgive you, my daughter."

Tanya jolted, glancing around, but only she and Clay were on the sun deck. She continued crying, but her tears had changed. They were no longer stinging poison but a warm shower. A pure sensation of relief overcame her. It flooded from her head to her toes, into her bones, relaxing her muscles, all over her skin, and deep, deep into her heart. It even reached her soul. Her soul rose, up, up, and up. It grew stupendously light.

Tanya felt overwhelmed with peace, a simple satisfying peace. *How am I allowed to feel this happy?* she asked herself. But the peace was so wonderful, why would she fight it? It was a gift from the one who loved her most. Tanya couldn't remember the last time she had felt so happy. *I want to feel like this every day for the rest of my life,* she thought. *From now on, I'm going to live in grace not in guilt.*

Suddenly a breath of laughter escaped her lips.

Clayton looked up. "What's so funny?"

"You know what, my son," said Tanya exuberantly, "I am proud of you and I love you."

Clayton's grin was as big as a watermelon, as bright as the sun. He stood up on the chair and embraced her. "I love you too, Mommy."

Cardinal Sabino Verdone experienced great pain in his knees as he descended the stairs to deck three. Oh, the price of age. Even though he agonized through the many stairs at the Vatican, Sabino had never grown accustomed to the havoc it caused his aging legs. He was not a fan of the spiraling grand

staircase inside the *Chrysalis*. The LED backlight
beneath the stone-inlaid steps was distracting.

Reaching deck three at last, Sabino limped past
the wine cellar on his left and the barred kitchen door
to his right. *Ah, there's the group,* he thought, spotting
Orlean, Ronald, the maid, the college girl, the
steward, and the awkward teenager gathered together
by the couches. *I think I'll join them.*

And then he saw the cupcakes—a platter of a
baker's dozen—right there in the middle of the
indoor dining table. *Chocolate, my favorite!* It would
seem that the icing was made of coffee, sprinkled with
black and white flecks. Perfectly scrumptious! Sabino
felt guilty as he plucked one from the plate. He had
always been overly fond of sweets. But today he
deserved it. He had just assisted Mrs. Jennings in a
heart-rending confession. This would be his reward.
He took a bite.

"Don't eat that!" the college girl was saying,
scurrying up to him.

Sabino chewed his bite and swallowed politely
before responding. "Ah, Shanlee, it's quite a delicious
cupcake. Coffee-flavored icing and something gooey
in the center. You should try one."

"No!" Shanlee gasped. "Don't eat anymore!
Please! The chef just set it on the table. We can't trust
him! We all believe that he is the murderer!"

Sabino steadied himself on the arm of the sofa.

Orlean approached him. "How do you feel,
brother?"

"I feel fine. Just a little shocked at the news," said Sabino. But he didn't feel fine. His throat was burning. His stomach was turning over in a violent protest. "I-I just think I need to sit down. The room is getting so small...."

Orlean screamed as Sabino collapsed to the ground, his mouth foaming with chocolate death.

16

The Past

Fifteen-year-old Connor watched his father receive news about his mother's condition on a dark spring evening. "The swelling in the brain has increased," said the balding doctor. "We would like your permission to operate immediately. If this continues any longer, she may not last the night."

Mr. Alekseev nodded. "Do whatever you need to, Doctor."

The doctor stepped away in a flash of blue scrubs.

Mr. Alekseev dropped his face into his hands and proceeded to rub his cheeks, forehead, nose and chin—again and again—like a song on repeat. "God, please save my wife. Please God. I'm not ready to say goodbye. I need her. God, I need her…."

Earlier in the day, Mrs. Alekseev had made final statements to her children, in her groggy frame of mind. She said things like "I love you," "Take care of each other," and "Your dad will need some extra help." Connor and his siblings tried to dismiss the phrases as the babblings of a sick person. But the statements had affected them nonetheless.

Connor escaped from the hospital waiting room, slumping to the floor in a corner by a vending machine. He often found solace in corners. But this time Connor was rapidly forming a survival plan. His dad was unusually emotional, his siblings were grieving, and it appeared that his mother was dying. What was he going to do?

I'll call Mrs. Stonewell, Connor decided. So he picked up his small flip-phone and dialed her contact.

"Well, hello, Connor. How are you?" said the pleasant voice of Andalucía Stonewell.

"Could be better, honestly," Connor replied.

"Oh no. I'm sorry. But I'm sure it will get better. You'll get through this, Connor. I know it. I wasn't going to tell you this just yet, but I'm organizing a group who will bring you meals this week. People will be stopping by. And besides, you can call me like this anytime you need to. Okay? I'm here for you."

"Thank you, Mrs. Stonewell. I really, really appreciate that."

The phone conversation went well. Despite the grim state of things, she was able to make Connor smile. Mrs. Stonewell was, at her core, a goofball. She had an uproarious sense of humor that was medicine for the soul on that dark night. She was also compassionate and knew when to utilize a weighty tone of voice. Connor was greatly cheered. In that moment, he decided that Andalucía Stonewell and her son Blake were the two people he trusted most in the entire world.

The graduates were like drapes of navy blue as they lined up in the lobby just outside the auditorium, eagerly awaiting their cue. Chief among them was Blake Stonewell—tall, handsome, and skinny, the pride and joy of his parents. Contrasting sharply with the caps and gowns of the graduates, Connor wore the bright-red volunteer T-shirt of the Nevada Society of Homeschool Families.

"Oh man, you look nervous," said fifteen-year-old Connor, tromping up to Blake. "Can I take a picture of you?"

"Sure," said Blake, displaying his playful and kindhearted grin. "But make it quick, if you don't mind. We're about to go on."

"Oh, it's fine. I'm a volunteer. I'll open the door for you guys." Connor snapped a few pictures with his ancient flip-phone. Vaguely, in the back of his mind, he wondered why he was the only one taking pictures of the graduates. But Connor was not especially attuned with implicit social customs.

"Hey, so now that I'm in JROTC, I need to get a part-time job. Then I can be even more like you!"

Blake smiled, but just for a moment. "I'm not the greatest guy in the world, Connor. You should know that."

"Psh...You're just being modest, as usual."

"And now, the senior class!" called the announcer from within the auditorium.

"Okay, it's time," said Connor as he opened the doors, assisted by another teenager in red. Connor watched this graduation with particular interest. Each celebrated senior brought a new possibility for the future as the announcer described their positive traits and dreams to the crowd.

It had been a wonderful day at the conference, the most social time of his year. Things were going well between him and the Stonewells. Ever since Connor's mother had left the hospital, the Stonewells had not once checked-in about Connor's issues. He almost wished they had, because he had been doing well for over a month.

The conference was like a family reunion, uniting homeschoolers from all over the state on their common ground of faith and values. Mrs. Stonewell had been friendly and approachable; she was like a fun aunt with whom Connor could discuss both silly and serious topics. She was the perfect substitute mother while Connor's mom recovered from brain surgery.

Blake was like his cool older cousin, and Connor looked up to him more than ever. Connor was proud to have acne on his face because he wanted to be like

Blake Stonewell. He wished he was taller and skinnier because he wanted to be like Blake Stonewell. He tucked his T-shirt into his jeans, despite how unfashionable it really was, because he wanted to be like Blake Stonewell. He would have founded the Blake Stonewell fan club, if fan clubs had been a social norm in the community.

Connor had recently confided to Blake about his crush on Joy Greenwood. Blake was doubtful that it would work, but Connor was hopeful. Joy wore denim skirts that reached her ankles, she styled her waist-length sheet of brown hair with a couple delicate elvish braids, and she discussed a variety of intellectual topics with remarkable aptitude. His liking must have shown because Joy gave him the nickname "Mr. Smiley" after one of their conversations. Connor dreamed of one day marrying Joy Greenwood and forever being close friends with the Stonewells. It was a glorious dream, sure to bring love and togetherness for many years.

17

Connor observed the impressionistic painting of a bearded man above the fireplace as he waited in the lounge on deck three with Najah, Orlean, Tanya, Ronald, Shanlee, Clay, and Durand. All were quietly preoccupied by their thoughts or simply remained silent, for the cardinal's death had shaken them. Preston had told them to stay in one place. He said it would be safest. Connor wasn't sure. He hated waiting because it made him feel useless. He wanted to do something instead of sitting in silence for hours. He felt like he was waiting to die.

Connor was sure that the pink paper caterpillar was meant to symbolize a woman, whom the murderer intended for his or her next victim. But the cardinal had just died! Surely, the cardinal was not the intended victim. Which of the four women did the murderer want to kill?

Connor looked toward Shanlee, who sat in the chair beside him. She had such a kind, innocent, yet captivating face. She was very beautiful, with her sleek black hair, unblemished skin, and perfectly oval face. But her beauty was not merely outward. Her presence was like the presence of compassion itself; her aura was unconditional forgiveness. Connor felt healing coming to him just by sitting near her, by glancing at her face. He wanted to do something for her.

He couldn't help but consider the question: *Did the murderer want to kill Shanlee?* He dreaded the thought. *No! The murderer can't kill her! I won't let it happen!* Connor searched his mind for any way he could save her. He wanted to stay with her every moment and personally ensure that she made it through the night, but he knew that people would grow suspicious if he did. Orlean and Ronald were certain that the chef was the murderer now. Connor had witnessed the chef place the cupcakes on the table with his own eyes. He must have killed the cardinal! But had he murdered the others too? The only problem was that the chef had been snoring in the bunk below him last night when Brock had been shot in the bridge deck. Surely Connor and Shanlee would have heard the chef go up the staircase when they were in the library last night. It was unlikely that the chef had slipped out. But it was possible.

He glanced at Ronald, who was frowning severely while silencing hiccups by squashing them down into his flabby neck. Was Ronald the murderer? It was possible. Ronald didn't seem to care for anyone. Connor could easily tell that Ronald was only on this trip to get something from Lady Cavenaugh, probably money. Connor got the feeling that Ronald didn't approve of him, but he didn't seem to approve of anyone except for Orlean, not even the extended family he had invited. Ronald had been very upset and nervous ever since the dead captain was discovered yesterday. Connor thought that he overdid it a bit, as if he were acting. Yes, Ronald was a possible suspect. Maybe he would benefit from Orlean's death. Maybe killing the captain and Brock Minton and sabotaging the equipment were just ploys to direct suspicion away from himself. Few people would suspect that a big businessman like Ronald Jennings would cut off all communication with the mainland.

Or maybe Lady Cavenaugh herself was the murderer. Connor observed how she tremulously poured more white wine into the goblet in her hand. Maybe she hadn't intended for her brother to die. Or maybe she was just pretending to be sad. What was she thinking about? Was she planning her next murder behind those dreary, aching eyes? Connor thought she was ridiculous to suggest that the captain had committed suicide. She couldn't say that anymore with Brock dead. *Was* she the murderer? It seemed less and less likely the more Connor considered the possibility. Orlean wouldn't kill her own captain, and her chief officer, and then sabotage all of the equipment in her own multi-million-dollar yacht. Would she? Connor remained uncertain because Orlean looked completely miserable as she drank sip after sip of her 1978 pinot grigio.

What about fifteen-year-old Durand? He was sitting there reading a book titled *The Sword in the Opal Sea.* He seemed like an innocent kid. But was he really? Connor decided it was very unlikely that he was a killer. It was more likely that he was just another socially awkward teenager.

He watched Shanlee tilt her eyes at the fire curiously. What was *she* thinking? Connor decided to end the silence.

He cleared his throat and everyone looked at him.

"Yes?" Orlean demanded.

"I just wanted to start some conversation." Connor saw kind affirmation in Shanlee's face. "It would help to calm the atmosphere."

Orlean frowned as if offended. "All right, but only whisper. This is the worst day of my life, Connor. Respect that." After a moment she directed her face back to the waves.

Shanlee smiled lightly. "Hi."

"Hey," Connor responded. They exchanged encouragement through their eyes.

"Thank you for saying that," Tanya said in desperate relief, placing her hand on her collarbone and shaking her head as she leaned closer to him. "I felt like I would scream if we remained silent a moment longer."

"No problem. I was thinking the same thing," Connor replied. They whispered short laughs only to relieve the weight that all three felt.

"My husband has been gone for hours now. I can't help but worry about him...." Her voice disappeared under stress and emotion.

"Don't worry. I'm sure he's all right. It's not dark yet." Connor noticed dimming twilight outside. He glanced back at Shanlee's understanding but concerned face.

"What do you think of the painting?" she asked.

Connor appreciated the change of subject and glanced at it for a moment. In various shades of black, gray and blue, the large canvas oil painting depicted an old man with a long twisting beard. In his beard were sea shells, starfish and gnarled barnacles. The eyes were deep, cold and powerful. "I don't know. I think I would like it if I understood it better."

"Yeah." Shanlee smiled warmly. "I wonder who it is? But that's how art is most of the time. You don't necessarily understand it. You just know that you like it or not. I love that painting. It's so mystical and intriguing."

"Yeah." Connor smiled also. "I can see the appeal."

"It's Neptune, you fools!" Orlean interjected.

"Oh, okay. That makes sense," Connor responded calmly.

"He must be furious with someone on board my yacht," Orlean seethed. "The gods are punishing us now! Oh, what have we done to provoke their wrath?" She chugged the last few sips of her wine and closed her eyes.

Shanlee turned back to Connor. "Did I ever ask where you went to college?"

"No, I went to college in Virginia," said Connor. "You said you're in college, right?"

"Yes, I am."

"She's in her junior year and she's only nineteen," Tanya stated proudly.

Connor was amazed. "That's impressive! You're very mature for your age."

Shanlee blushed. "Thank you. A lot of people say that. I think it's partly because I was homeschooled."

Connor made a vow to himself. *I will not let her die. I will not let this wonderful young woman die. No matter what it takes, I will protect her.*

Mrs. Jennings gasped as she looked toward the stairs and rose from her seat. The seven others did the same, knowing what she saw. Preston entered with an expression of deepest gravity, his shoulders sloped with concern.

"Well, did you find out anything?" Ronald asked in a husky voice.

"I did learn a few things, but nothing yet that would form a decisive conclusion." Preston extended his arm as his wife rushed to him.

"Well, you certainly took your time," said Tanya, expressing her worry while she held him closely.

"I have to be thorough." He looked at Connor. "Mr. Alekseev, you are rooming with Mr. Leveque, correct?"

"Yes," Connor replied, grimacing.

"Then you might want to consider taking Brock Minton's old quarters into your occupation. Since he didn't die there, it would be suitable. You would be wise not to spend the night in the chef's room, considering the present circumstances."

Connor nodded. "I agree."

"What about you, Preston?" Ronald growled, ready to snap at anything Preston said or did. "Why aren't you being so 'wise'? How do you know your wife hasn't killed them? Maybe *you* should consider 'the present circumstances.' "

Tanya gasped again, but now with fright while Preston shot his brother such a look—a look of reproach and shame. Ronald had always hated the way Preston took control of situations.

"Now," Preston began. "After we saw what happened today, we can no longer consume any of the food that Mr. Leveque prepares. However, we all must eat. I found a container of cold sandwiches in the bar refrigerator downstairs, which should suffice as dinner. Otherwise, I suggest that we make our way to our staterooms as quickly as possible. Be sure to lock your doors and windows."

After selecting wax-paper-wrapped sandwiches from the bar on deck two, the group dispersed. Ronald Jennings stomped down the art-lined hallway toward their staterooms, addressing his brother. "You and your favorites, Preston! What do you mean advising Connor to move into the chief officer's room? You favor the steward above the rest, and you know it! What makes you so sure he isn't the murderer?"

Preston turned to his brother. "Mr. Leveque clearly poisoned the cardinal to death this afternoon. We all need protection from him. If Mr. Leveque departs from the kitchen tonight, he might try assaulting Mr. Alekseev in their room. Although I have not completely crossed him off of the list of suspects, I have no reason to believe that Mr. Alekseev is the murderer."

Ronald was more irritated at this reply than anything else and marched into his VIP suite with a huff, unable to stand his brother's presence any longer. Orlean Cavenaugh had already gone upstairs to her master suite on deck three.

"Are you sure you don't want to sleep on the floor in our room, Shanlee?" Mrs. Jennings asked tenderly while she laid her daughter's sandwich on the nightstand.

"No, I'll be fine in here for the night. Please don't worry. I'll put a chair under the door for extra security." Shanlee tried to comfort her mother but failed, for what mother could be comforted so easily in times of such deadly threats?

"Secure your window thoroughly," Preston instructed. "Take extra precautions. Be suspicious of everything."

A cold disquiet rushed over Shanlee's skin as if an unknown sea creature had slid around her ankle, leaving slimy spots. "It's so horrible, what happened to the cardinal."

"Oh yes, it's unbelievable." Tanya shuddered. "But I'm sure he's in heaven with the Lord. He was a very kind man."

"Yes, he was," Preston affirmed passively, releasing the words like three remote leaves floating on salty waves. "Now we must return to our room and reconvene with the boys. We will meet you at the table tomorrow at seven. Your mother and I will pray together tonight."

Mrs. Jennings hugged her daughter, and they both bid her goodnight.

The door to the master suite pried open just an inch—and then stopped. After a minute, it opened all the way. Orlean Cavenaugh emerged wearing a white cashmere bathrobe she had purchased in Sri Lanka many years ago. Holding her breath, she tiptoed past the kitchen and her glowing museum of wine. The light was still on in the kitchen.

She climbed the stone inlaid steps, ascending to deck four.

Once she reached the sliding glass door that led to the outdoor dining area, Orlean halted. She gazed beyond the glass. A star managed to stare back at her, but suddenly it was overtaken by her own domineering reflection. Orlean was like a forlorn ghost hovering above the water, still and motionless in the dimming world. She was old, mottled, and, yes, ugly. Orlean felt as if she had never met this woman before, but this was herself—Orlean Cavenaugh, a fading corpse striving to appear beautiful with many futile attempts.

Orlean tugged open the door and hurried up the exterior steps on the side of the boat, which led to the sun deck. Steadying herself carefully with sure footing, Orlean pulled and pulled at the cover on top of the hot tub. This was why she hired staff. Connor should be doing this. But no matter. She wasn't going to wake up anyone tonight. Leveraging the full weight of her body, Orlean finally succeeded at moving the cursed cover. An aquamarine glow shone upon her as she slipped into the hot, soothing water.

She was ugly. Orlean wondered how she had been unable to clearly see this before. She remembered how she would always thrust the thought away, retreating from reality by telling herself that she was better than others because of her money or her title. Lady Cavenaugh—it was a beautiful title. Even if her face didn't quite match, her name was what made her great.

She noticed the dark spots of melanoma on her arms. Like the sudden crash of a fine vase, all the strength her title seemed to hold and all the superiority faded into nothingness. It was as if she had been exalting a grand and glorious monarch butterfly, setting it on a pedestal with idealistic fantasies, but then realized it was just a dusty moth. She expected a shock, and she did feel somewhat shocked, but she realized in the back of her mind that she had known it all along.

Oh, how enraged she was! Why had everyone lied to her? Deceiving and flattering her as if she were a goddess, telling her, "Oh, how beautiful you are," "You are the kindest woman I have ever met," "You are just gorgeous." They were all lies—blatant, cruel fantasies. She hated flattery.

But wait, wasn't that how she had acquired her fortune and title? Orlean remembered the day in her youth (nineteen, wasn't it?) when she was visiting Paris with her aunt and uncle. Her uncle had done a favor for some upper-class person, and they were invited to that grand party as a token of appreciation. She recalled how excited she had been, chatting happily with her aunt about how fine the clothes, the food, and the people would be. Then the party came. Sometimes handsome young lords see women as less than human, as something to use, to enjoy, and to captivate; they like to play with innocent hearts like new, intriguing toys. Orlean remembered how she ran off with a young man named Lord Cavenaugh without a second thought, dreaming of living forever with him in his enormous mansion. But two weeks after their marriage, she discovered how unfaithful a handsome young lord could really be.

She murdered him by electrocuting the pool when he was swimming one night. She had been in a rage—a mindless, unthinking rage. It was the haunting sin. But of course, she did it! Any other woman who knew that men and women were equal would have done the same. Wouldn't they? After all, she had given up everything for the handsome young lord Cavenaugh. And what had he given her? He probably would have cast Orlean aside in a year or two. Orlean just had to take his fortune and title for herself.

Yes, it was perfectly understandable and so very sad. Anyone who truly understood the story would have felt terribly sorry for her. But of course, she never told anyone. It would be mistaken for a confession. Orlean Cavenaugh was not sorry for what she had done. She was sorry for how sad and lonely the rest of her life had been.

Orlean nearly died of fear when she heard a thump behind her. Splashing like a cornered dolphin, she scanned back and forth along the sun deck. She squinted at the lounge chairs, the stairwell, and the dark, vast ocean. If only she had brought her glasses.

Orlean decided that she was a foolish sitting duck up here by herself and returned to the master suite.

18

The morning was still. The yacht barely rocked. Two bedside lamps glowed. Connor, Ronald, Tanya and Preston awaited Lady Cavenaugh's reply. She looked down at the body, struggling to believe. Atop the indoor table on deck three was a pink paper butterfly, a white page with writing, and the cardinal's body propped up in a chair. Preston handed her the paper, and she read:

Keep your scarlet,
Keep your White.
Pricy male,
Fade to mark the night.

The deceiver smiled,
The deceiver told,
"No, I'm not bad.
Don't be so bold."

"I haven't raped,
I haven't seduced."

Now talk of hope,
Twist, blind, and bruise.

Didn't you want this?
Didn't death appeal?
Talk of conversion now
Doesn't it mean 'to heal'?

Hate is my gift,
Take it, don't frown.
If only I could give you,
the cold hard ground.
—The Glass Shadow

Lady Cavenaugh removed her eyes from the page and stared at the motionless body. "How cruel to put his body in the chair like that." She bit her lip. "Xenon! Xenon has done this!" Filled with a shaking rage, she turned to Preston. "We must bring justice. Today!"

Connor clicked on the light at the poolside bar on deck two, early at 9:00 a.m., as the four others approached. Lady Cavenaugh ambled up, very ghost-like, and managed to lift herself onto a barstool.

"I think I'll go check on the children," said Tanya Jennings, heading for the grand staircase.

"Make me a scotch on the rocks," Ronald demanded grimly.

"Would you like a drink, ma'am?" Connor asked, standing in front of the fountain mirror while he removed a hanging glass.

"I'll have a cappuccino with three shots of espresso," she replied, rubbing her temples.

"Yes, ma'am." Connor loaded the espresso machine with fresh coffee beans. "Anything for you, sir?" he asked Preston.

"Just water," Preston whispered.

"Connor, I thought I was able to trust Xenon," said Lady Cavenaugh in a slow, cold voice. "I trusted him for fifteen years. Yes, sometimes he made crude comments. I always hated his vile sense of humor. But"—she smacked her frail hand on the counter—"but what he did, poisoning my brother!" Her entire body was trembling now. "He must pay. I will bring vengeance on him!"

Preston's graying hair was perfectly parted on the right side, just as always, the exposed line of scalp like a straight line of logic. "It is very disrespectful what was done to Mr. Verdone's body today, moving him like a dummy." He sighed heavily. "However, I must clarify that we do not know for certain that Xenon is the murderer."

"Yes, we do!" Ronald huffed. "We watched the chef emerge from the kitchen and put that plate of poisoned cupcakes onto the dining table. We saw it with our own eyes."

Orlean and Connor both expressed their confirmation.

"You just want to be right, don't you?" Ronald accused.

Preston lifted his head above the comment. "Okay, thank you for confirming your eyewitness accounts. Most likely, the chef poisoned the cupcakes, which resulted in Mr. Verdone's death. However, he might not have committed the other murders. Connor here confirmed that he heard the chef snoring the night on which Brock was killed."

As Connor passed the white ceramic cup and saucer to Lady Cavenaugh, she suddenly removed the saucer and hurled it onto the floor. It shattered with a resounding crash. The speech and movements of the Jennings brothers halted.

"Shut up you two! I don't care!" Lady Cavenaugh breathed rapidly, taking sip after sip of the cappuccino. "I don't care if you think Xenon killed the others or not. I want to destroy him. I will destroy him! He utterly betrayed us all." She directed her bloodshot eyes at the three men in turn. "Are you going to help me or not?"

Preston and Ronald pondered silently. But Connor didn't need any more time. "I have an idea."

Xenon Leveque casually began making the soup. Skillfully he sliced carrots, onions, and tomatoes. Even though it clicked and squirmed in protest, he dropped a living lobster into a pot of boiling water. He sniffled and wiped his nose with the back of his hand, his sickly eyes peering out above his white goatee like two glowing eels.

All these stupid murders, he thought. *I almost wish they hadn't happened so I could get more sleep.* He smiled at this wicked thought and became a bit careless with his hands. While he tasted some of the creation, he spilled a spoonful on the stove, causing a chorus of sizzling. The smell of burnt seafood wafted through the air. The chef cursed and resumed his work with a grimace.

A knock rattled the kitchen door.

Xenon took out his sharp meat cleaver. "What?"

"It's Connor. I have your Armani suit. The others are going through your stuff, but I managed to sneak this out. I'll give you the suit in exchange for some food."

The suit was worth almost five thousand dollars. Xenon thought it was a good deal. "All right." He began moving the stainless steel table he had used to bar the door.

He slowly opened the door, eyeing Connor's face through the window. "All right. Just slip—"

Connor raised a fire extinguisher, doused Xenon, and barged through the door.

"Ahhh!" the chef cried, falling backwards. The knife clattered on the ground.

Connor jumped onto the shocked chef, but he slipped away.

Xenon scrambled to his feet and reclaimed the meat cleaver. "You're not getting me so easily!" He rushed to the pot of boiling water. Using a cup measure, he scooped out a large portion of water. With one sudden fling of his arm, Xenon hurled the boiling water right at Connor's face.

Connor dropped to the floor and slid to the side, barely dodging the burning spray, which splashed on the floor behind him.

The chef wiped the white powder out of his eyes, putting his left foot back, as if ready for a knife fight.

Crouched in a prepared stance, Connor brandished the fire extinguisher and charged. He swung it at the chef's hand, knocking the knife out.

"Don't hurt me!"

While the chef cradled his wounded hand, Connor seized the opportunity. He hurled the chef to the ground, pinning him down with his knee.

"Preston! Now!"

Preston rushed in, with duct tape in his hands.

"Don't hurt me!" the chef demanded.

"Mr. Xenon Leveque," Preston said as Connor wrapped the duct tape around the chef's wrists, "you are under arrest for the murder of Cardinal Sabino Verdone."

"Who do you think you are? You're not the police in any country!"

"No, I'm not," said Preston. "But the rules are different at sea. However, I am a lawyer in the United States of America."

Orlean Cavenaugh hesitantly entered the kitchen. "Did you get the mutinous villain?"

"Yes, we did," Connor replied, walking the chef out of the galley.

"Where are you taking me?" Xenon murmured.

"You will be confined to your stateroom," Preston declared. "We will keep a man on guard outside your room until we reach land."

Orlean Cavenaugh lurched forward, clutching the chef's collar with shaking hands. "Where did you put the radio? Where are the international cell phones?"

The chef began to cackle as if this was the most amusing question he had ever heard. But he didn't say another word.

Ronald Jennings puffed an expensive Cuban cigar as he leaned against the railing on the pool deck with Preston, Connor, and Orlean. They watched the yellow sun plunge into the orange waves. Najah Hasan was standing guard at the chef's door.

"We have to find the radio!" Ronald coughed gruffly. "You don't think he tossed our cell phones overboard, do you?"

"I sure hope not," Connor said. "I still have mine, but I haven't had any service since we left New York."

"Your cell phone is probably not equipped to connect with the satellites in space," Preston remarked. "Mine can. But unfortunately it is missing."

Orlean shuddered, taking a good sip of her French Chardonnay. "I wouldn't put it past the little devil. But we must find some form of communication with the outside world." A wave of exhaustion overcame Orlean. She touched her head. "I must retire to my bedroom. Please, all of you, search the *Chrysalis* for a functioning radio or an international cell phone or anything that we can use to communicate."

Ronald dropped his cigar overboard without a second thought. "Oh no, Orlean! Let me accompany you. I'll find you some painkillers."

"I'm fine, Ronald. I just need a few moments alone."

"Well, at least let me walk you to your room," Ronald persisted as their voices faded away.

Tall and stately, Preston held his hands behind his back and cleared his throat. "Well, Mr. Alekseev, you certainly proved yourself today. Thank you for helping us. May I ask, where did you learn to fight like that?"

Connor shrugged. "I took martial arts pretty seriously for about a year when I was in high school. I guess it just came right back."

Preston frowned. "But you reacted so quickly. You haven't practiced since then?"

"Maybe a little," Connor admitted. "I was fighting to save our lives. That's a powerful motivator."

"Yes. Yes, it is." Preston grinned genially. "Well, I think I'm going to find my wife. She's making a new pot of soup. There will be no poison in this one. Would you mind beginning the search of the yacht?"

Later in the evening, Connor's search was not going well. He had been through every single cabinet in the yacht. He had searched the captain's stateroom and Brock's stateroom. He had scoured the kitchen, the laundry room, and the utility room. Where was the radio or the international cell phones? As Connor stopped to turn on the light in the dining room on deck three, he noticed a bright-orange paper caterpillar on the polished wood. He released a slow, troubled breath. He had to tell the others. But maybe not yet. Now wasn't the time for more bad news.

19

The Past

Fifteen-year-old Connor forced a chipped plastic cup off the stack and filled it with cafeteria lemonade. He lifted his tray and headed for a table.

Tall and cheerful, Blake Stonewell passed Connor and said, "Hey Parrot! How's it going?"

Connor rushed away without responding.

Connor, Blake, and about a hundred other homeschooled teenagers were attending a summer leadership camp, hosted by a local college. It was a three-day adventure where you stayed in the dorm rooms, attended motivational and instructive sessions, and played exhilarating outdoor games like the ever-popular ultimate frisbee. Unfortunately, the night before the camp began, Connor had watched inappropriate videos online. His heart was gripped by a cruel shame that refused to let him recover.

The issue was that the Stonewells expected Connor to be free, to never view inappropriate content online again. Only then would he be allowed to hang out with Blake one-on-one as a friend. Norman, Andalucía, and Blake were all under the impression that Connor had been on a winning streak. What would happen if they found out? Connor shuddered to think of it. He had a problem of being completely honest with Blake. Therefore, here at the camp, Connor was avoiding him.

He chose a table with one of his roommates, a gawky young man with tucked-in plaid shirts, overly gelled hair, and a vacant expression. "Hey, Tucker," Connor started chatting. "What did you think of the last session?"

"Oh, it was great."

Blake Stonewell approached the table, tray in hand. "Can I sit with you guys?"

"Sure, Blake! Please join us!" Tucker said, hustling to remove his overloaded backpack from a plastic chair.

Connor refused to acknowledge Blake. "So, Tucker, the session, what did you think?"

"Oh yeah, I loved it. Dr. Stormfair is an excellent..." His voice trailed away as he noticed Connor's rude behavior.

"I really liked it," said Blake. "What about you, Connor?"

Throughout the entire meal, Connor persistently looked away from Blake. And Blake certainly noticed.

By the time the last session of the camp was starting, Connor was feeling remorseful. Lo and behold, Blake moved over to sit next to him. "I'm sorry for not talking to you earlier at lunch," Connor said in a heavy tone.

"It's okay. I forgive you," Blake responded. "But are you doing okay?"

It was a question that threatened to reveal the truth—a truth that could forever destroy Connor's friendship with Blake. "No, I'm not doing great," said Connor, and the session began.

During the session, all Connor could think about was how he wanted to break free from the clutches of this cruel shame. He simply couldn't tell his dad. No way! He couldn't stand the look of sinking disappointment that had appeared on his father's face the first time he told his dad about his issues. And he couldn't tell his mother because she was still recovering from brain surgery. He considered telling Mrs. Stonewell, but that would be challenging since she had been so friendly with Connor recently and he didn't want to ruin that. However, opening up to Blake had brought relief in the past. Why not now?

Connor tossed and turned in his bed at home that night. He had to tell someone! And he still felt guilty for his rude treatment of Blake at the camp. He had to explain everything. He just had to.

Quiet as a mouse, Connor tiptoed down the hallway. The shadows were dark and discouraging,

hopeless and taunting, as Connor sat down at the
living room computer, logged in to his email, and
began typing.

Dear Blake,

*I'm really sorry for how I treated you at leadership camp. I
shouldn't have ignored you like that. I feel horrible about it. But
there's something you don't know. I haven't been doing well
lately. The night before the camp, I watched some bad videos on
the internet. I'm sorry. I know your parents expected me to stop
looking at inappropriate content or we couldn't hang out
anymore. I think this means we have to stop being friends now.
If we keep hanging out, I might hurt you. And I really don't
want to do that.*

I'm going to miss you, my friend.

Sincerely,

Connor

"Oh no! Oh no! What have I done?" Connor
asked himself as he jolted out of bed the
next morning and ran for his flip-phone. He had to
call Blake and explain over the phone. Maybe he
could still fix what he had said. Blake was an
understanding guy.

Connor dialed once, then twice, then three times.
But no answer. Just when Connor was trying to
predict what would happen next, he looked at the

screen of his ringing phone. Blake Stonewell was calling back.

"Hey, Connor," said Blake in a serious voice.

Oh no. The damage had already been done. "Hi Blake, did you read my email?"

"You mean the one from last night? Yes, I did."

"I'm sorry. I shouldn't have said those things. I wrote it late at night when I was feeling really depressed. I think we can still be friends. I do want to be an honorable man. I think, with time, I could be a good influence on you."

"Late at night, huh? Okay, that explains some things." Blake sighed. "Thank you for trusting me. But I don't know what to do. Can I show the email to my parents?"

Connor had expected this question. Blake always discussed important topics with his parents. But Mr. Stonewell was the one who had insisted that Connor must stop viewing inappropriate content in order to be Blake's friend. What would happen? Despite his fears, Connor said, "Okay, you can tell them."

That night, Mr. and Mrs. Alekseev called a private meeting with their son. Their postures were unusually formal as they sat across from Connor at the dining room table. The sinking disappointment that Connor dreaded so much was on his father's face, and his mother looked very sad. This was bad. He was in deep trouble now.

"Connor, did you send this email?" Mr. Alekseev passed a sheet of paper across the table.

"Yes. I did," Connor admitted.

Mr. Alekseev grimaced, taking a couple hefty breaths. "I just got off the phone with Norman Stonewell." He glanced at Mrs. Alekseev. "Your mother and I have discussed it and we have agreed that you can't go to Junior ROTC for a month."

He was grounded for a month. That wasn't so bad. "Okay. But what did Mr. Stonewell say?"

Mr. Alekseev rubbed his face, forehead, nose, and chin again and again, just like he had when Mrs. Alekseev was in the hospital. And then he lowered his hands. "The Stonewells are extremely upset. They said you can never again be friends with Blake."

Four months later, Connor strode down the sidewalk in the middle of the night. He didn't feel tired, even though the autumn moon shone in the highest point of the blackness. Silently, without disturbing his family, he had gathered his things and waited for the hours to pass. Once the uncomfortable glow of the clock read 2:30, Connor slipped out the side door and began his walk. The wind held a chill like a warning of danger ahead. With each quick step, Connor knew he was getting closer and closer to what his father had forbidden him to do. He hoped his sticky note, reading, "I'm out walking," would convince his parents of what wasn't the full truth. Connor was determined to talk with Blake at a volunteer event.

A flag snapped and rippled somewhere in the windy darkness as Connor sat on an illuminated trailer step, waiting for Blake while the other volunteers from JROTC chatted and sipped black coffee. He declined the offer for a free glazed doughnut. At last, a tall young man in a navy-blue hoodie and a frayed baseball cap saw Connor but proceeded to the sign-in table. Connor went up to him.

"Hey, Blake, I need to talk to you."

Blake finished his writing and faced Connor in a way like disappointment. "Then say it."

"I have to talk to you privately."

Blake stuffed his hands into his hoodie pocket. "What's wrong with right here?"

"Please, it's very important. Please."

"All right."

The gravel crunched beneath their feet as the two teenagers walked away from the trailer and the people around it. They stopped at a row of parked cars.

"Okay, we're alone. What did you want to say?"

Connor took a deep breath, then launched into it. "This situation of you guys rejecting me—it's really hard! It's destroying me. I don't know how to get through it. I don't know if I can overcome this."

"You can move forward, bro. There's a bright future ahead of you."

"No, Blake! It's not that simple!" Connor held up his hands like two stop signs. "Please hear me out. There is a way to resolve this."

Blake stood taller. "I'm sorry Connor, but we can't be friends. There have to be consequences. The thoughts you talked about were a big deal. A thought is the birthplace of an action."

"But not every thought becomes an action. Sometimes they're just thoughts that pass away! What about you? Have you acted out every thought you've ever had?"

Reluctantly Blake shook his head.

"See! There is something very wrong here! And it's tearing me apart!" Connor spoke with a tone of potent entreaty, each word saturated in grief. "Look! Look at the harm that was caused! Because of an email that I wrote to you back in June, our families are no longer friends. This is a bigger deal than just our friendship falling apart. I didn't realize this would have such a harmful effect! Did you notice that this was the first summer in like three years when you guys didn't come over for a day at my family's house?"

Blake nodded. "Yes, I noticed."

"Because of what I wrote, because of the words I said, several friendships have been affected by this.

My mom's friendship with your mom, your friendship with my brother, my sister's friendship with your mother and your sisters. And my friendship with your mom." Connor's voice broke, but he pulled himself together. "She was like a second mother to me."

Blake's amber eyes scanned the distance, a flicker of change appearing. "It is sad. I'm going to miss your family. I'm going to miss you too, Parrot." He brightened. "I'm even going to miss your many questions."

Connor's heart was too heavy to be lifted by the comment. "Then help me fix this! It's wrong. It shouldn't be this way! Why can't we go back to the way things were at the leadership camp, back when you came over and sat next to me? Don't you see, Blake! A terrible harm was done and it's all my fault! But it's fixable. It is!"

Blake stood as if on a fence, not moving forward or backward, just holding a firm position in the middle. "Words have power. You can't just take back what you said."

"I disagree!" Connor retorted. "If we can't retract our statements, how can we ever grow? How does anyone resolve conflict? Please listen! I wrote that email from a mindset of depression. There is lust in my heart. I admit it. There is. But I'm trying to get rid of it. I want to be an honorable man. That's why I wanted to hang out with you, Blake. Because I wanted to be like you. Isn't that what a big brother is?

Someone we look up to? And that's just how I see
you, okay? Please help me remove the lies and
replace them with the truth!"

Blake took off his frayed cap and fiddled with it
for a moment. "I would have to speak with my
parents before making a decision."

"What? No!" Connor's eyes widened fearfully.
"Please don't! The first time that happened, I was
grounded from hanging out with you one-on-one.
The second time, I was banned from being your
friend ever again. Can you just decide for yourself
this time?"

Blake sighed. "You can't ask me not to talk with
my parents. They are my best friends, my
counselors." He smiled. "They're a bit protective, but
they love me."

"A bit protective?" Connor took a step backward.
"Much more than that."

"Okay, true. They're really protective."

"Please, this time think it through yourself,
without their advice. What is the right course of
action? What will help to fix this horrible, depressing
situation?" Connor felt a surge of exhaustion. "Dude,
I'm really tired. Would you mind if I waited in your
truck while you volunteer at the event? I just need to
rest my eyes for a while."

Blake exhaled grumpily. "Okay. Sure."

They walked over to his dark-blue pickup.
Connor sat in the passenger seat, holding his face in
his hands. "Thanks for hearing me out."

"You're welcome." Blake stuffed the key back into his jeans pocket. "But no promises, okay?"

"Okay. Just think about what I said. Please."

Connor rested in Blake's truck for about an hour while the sun crept over the arid mountains. There was hope! This was why Connor liked talking to Blake, because he truly listened; he actually considered what Connor had to say. Maybe things would work out. Connor felt comforted in Blake's truck, with the helter-skelter tools in the back and the smell of concrete dust. Just being in his truck was a sign that things would get better.

But Blake tarried for a long time. The parking lot filled. The sun rose high above the mountains. Connor climbed out and returned to the trailer of refreshments for the volunteers. "Hey Frenchie, have you seen Blake Stonewell?" he asked another guy from JROTC. Frenchie pointed to the doughnut table.

Connor's face was bright with hope as he hurried over to Blake. "So, did you think about it?"

Blake refused to meet his eyes. "We can't be friends. I'm sorry. Oh, but there's your dad. I asked him to pick you up."

It was like a bucket of ice water was thrown over the valley. All hope of reconciliation with the Stonewell family was lost. Slowly Connor walked toward his father. Even from a distance he could tell that Mr. Alekseev was extremely worried.

20

Tanya Jennings prepared a twin mattress in the corner for Clayton to sleep on. She tucked in the last of the covers and fluffed up the pillow. "There you go."

Clayton jumped onto the bed, hitting the resistance of the hardwood floor faster than he expected. "Ow!"

"These beds aren't made to jump on, sweetie." She tucked him under the covers.

"Mommy, do you have an extra pair of earplugs? I lost mine again."

"Yes, I do." She handed him two lime-green ear plugs from her purse. He smiled excitedly, as if given a new toy.

Soon, Preston and Tanya were lying in their bed. The sounds of Clayton's heavy breathing and the rocking of the yacht droned methodically in the background. Tanya was glad that Durand had decided to sleep downstairs. It gave her more privacy, a chance to speak with Preston about her confession with the cardinal. She had to catch him before he dozed off.

"Um, Preston dear, are you still awake?"

"Yes. I am." He rolled onto his side and looked right at her.

Rarely did Tanya have her husband's full attention. He was usually preoccupied with thoughts of his cases at work, and he was a very fast sleeper. On this trip, Preston had been even more preoccupied, understandably so considering the horrible murders of three people. But now, at last, his ears and his mind were present at the same time. She had to seize the opportunity.

"Oh um. Yes, um…" Tanya became a little tongue-tied. Her nerves fluttered rapidly in her stomach. "Well, I just wanted to tell you that I had a truly transformative experience recently."

"Oh yeah? What's that?"

"Yesterday, before his passing, I went up to the sun deck with Mr. Verdone. I actually confessed something to him. It was, oh, it was just so amazing! I have never felt such alleviation in my life."

"Hmm, curious," said Preston. "Did he say the prayer of absolution over you?"

This wasn't the response she was hoping for. "Oh. What? I don't think so. Hmm. But then again, I wouldn't have recognized it, since, you know, we're Protestants."

Preston readjusted his position and closed his eyes as if assuming that Tanya had finished her story. "Well, I'm very glad you feel better."

"Yes. Me too."

Tanya's soul felt much better. But her marriage seemed to be worse than ever. She was suddenly confronted with the reality that Preston and Tanya had led very separate lives. They were devoted to each other, yes. They both believed in complete dedication to marriage. But Tanya felt as though they were cohabitants rather than intimates.

She recalled a time when she was driving home from the grocery store and passed two cop cars parked in such a way that their driver's-side windows were adjacent to one another. A few days later, she passed the same parking lot and the two cop cars were there once again. They must have been good friends. Tonight, however, Tanya had a horrible feeling that those two cops were closer with each other than she was with her own husband.

Tanya had lived a guilt-driven life. She adopted, raised children, and homeschooled, motivated by a stinging guilt that kept her very busy. She had tried to wipe away the sins of her past with good deeds, a toil that had proved fruitless. She had been like a hamster on a wheel, chasing a treat that was always out of reach no matter how fast she ran.

But now, her sins had been cleansed by the blood of Jesus Christ. She was relieved of a burden she had carried for many years. The redemption she had chased was at last in her heart. Tanya felt extremely grateful.

However, it was as though tinted glasses had fallen off her eyes. And she was grieved by some of the things she was seeing. Her marriage wasn't very intimate. This had to change! It had to. But how? Tanya resolved to revisit the topic with Preston another time, after they were safely off this dreadful yacht. Maybe she would even suggest marriage counseling.

Suddenly Tanya realized that she hadn't felt guilty for an entire day. She was flabbergasted. Could she actually be changing for the better? How remarkable! She thanked God in a silent prayer. As she drifted off to sleep, a peace washed over her that was the greatest gift she had received in many years.

"Enter!" said the voice of Orlean Cavenaugh. Connor opened the door to the master suite, a tray with a covered bowl in his right hand. "Here is your soup, ma'am."

"Set it on the coffee table and leave, please," came the muffled reply. Connor obeyed.

Orlean Cavenaugh peered out of the blue mosquito net that covered her king bed like an old zebra scrutinizing a clump of grass. Satisfied, she crawled out of bed. There lay the soup on her pale Japanese coffee table. She pulled up her long, dragging negligee so as not to trip and sat on the sofa. Exotic furs draped loosely on the cushions: mink, cheetah, tiger, and chinchilla. She placed the tray comfortably on her lap, picked up the spoon, and looked down into the bowl. Whatever cheer she was beginning to find was gone in a flash as a brutal depression overpowered her. Her shoulders slouched forward. A large, vile mosquito wormed around on the surface of the soup. She let out a long, encumbered sigh with the little breath she had inhaled. It was all real now. Sin, emptiness, destruction, ultimate death—they were real. She couldn't worship the idealistic glitter anymore. She couldn't remove the unpleasant from her life any longer. They were there and they were real.

She plunged the spoon into the orange blend and swirled the soup around, mixing the insect in thoroughly. She filled the spoon and swallowed the contents. It would have tasted the same, delicious, but she couldn't believe in its flavor anymore. Her tastebuds were deceivers now.

She forced herself to consume the entire bowlful. She hadn't eaten all day. This was her punishment— the consequence of the life for which she had asked. It was finally here. Death was here.

Scraped bare of its contents, the bowl went back on the coffee table. Orlean took a sip of water to wash out the taste and sighed again. She felt almost proud, as if she had suffered something that wasn't expected of her. She felt as if she had outsmarted those who had put the mosquito in her bowl, and they were now huddling together in the shadows at a loss about what to do next.

They? she thought. *Who are they?*

Ronald Jennings knocked on the door to the master suite. "It's me."

"Oh, Ronald. Please come in."

Ronald sat beside her, causing the entire sofa to shake. He touched her knee affectionately and gazed into her eyes with endearment, his practiced compassion coming out in a squashed grin. "Are you all right, Orlean?"

She turned away. "Oh, I don't know, Ron. Nothing is all right. I don't know what I'm feeling. It's all very horrible." The memory of who he was came to her, and she looked back at him. "But it doesn't matter. I was planning this trip to be my last, anyway."

"What do you mean?"

"I mean, this was the last trip that I was able to take in the yacht. I know you came to try to get money from me. Don't worry. I'm used to it. But the truth is, I'm broke."

"What?" Ronald removed his hand from her knee and inched away. "You're not serious, are you?"

"I only wish it was a joke. Yes, it's true. If I tried to pay off all my debts now with all my possessions, I would still have about two-thirds remaining unpaid. I am thoroughly broke. This trip was going to be my swan song to the extravagant life."

"What!" Ronald jumped to his feet with surprising agility for his stature. "You mean I did all this for nothing?" His eyes flared with anger as a drop of sweat trickled down the side of his face.

"Yes, I'm sorry, Ron. You must be very upset." Orlean looked up at him, not in the least surprised by his reaction. Ronald shook his head once in disbelief and turned quickly to leave.

Orlean was alone again.

She sat for a while, letting her mind wander, knocking on doors that hadn't been opened in ages, or noticing new truths from more recent events. After coming across the memory of her brother and then his death, she came back to herself and looked down at the forlorn bowl. The few traces of orange had dried into a smudged, yellowish shade. "I think I'll clear it," she told herself. A simple thought was refreshing.

Sound was absent from the yacht, save her pattering feet, but the iridescent lamps lining the hall seemed to say something very quiet and listless: "This is life. This is the world."

Deck three was empty. "Mrs. Jennings?" she called. No answer. *They must have returned to their rooms,* she thought and smiled weakly. *Ah well.*

The dinner table reflected the light from the dimmed chandelier, attracting Orlean's eyes. Something was on it. *What is that?* Leaning closer, she spotted an orange origami caterpillar. She lifted it and turned the paper in her hand, observing the clean folds. "Orange, orange—just like my soup." She placed it back on the wood and lifted her head slightly. "I am the orange. I am the threatened."

She walked over to a small stand that elevated a vase of tropical flowers. She reached around the back and removed a purposefully hidden bird-of-paradise flower; its petals were curled and wrinkled, and its bright-orange, youthful color had faded. Orlean clutched the flower to her bosom and slowly made her way to the grand staircase. She placed her feet on the stone-inlaid steps like a weary horse pulling a great load up a freezing hill.

The cold greeted Orlean as she stood beside the outside table on deck four. The wind seemed to say, "Come, my most gracious guest, and I will show you to your place of darkness where you will taste the delicacies of death, for we are feasting on it." She gazed out at the boundless ocean, entrapping her with loneliness and isolation. Some moonlight leaked through the shrouding black clouds, barely illuminating her surroundings.

With great care, she climbed the exterior staircase, to the sun deck on the very top of the yacht. She trod the wood to the far end of the boat—as if a hand led her. Steam rose from the dark Jacuzzi. *Someone left the cover off. Ah well. It doesn't matter now.*

She stepped in. The entire world was still.

The warm water didn't comfort Orlean like she thought it would. She looked over the bow at the dark ocean stretching far and forever. She wondered why she had purchased a yacht. She hated the ocean. It was a horrible vastness that reminded Orlean of the loneliness in her soul. Loneliness was her only loyal friend. Tears swelled in her eyes, but only one fell.

Before tonight the ocean was like her slave and she was a goddess, cruising her seven-sea realm whenever she pleased. The *Chrysalis* was her throne and palace. But now she discovered the truth; it was all an illusion. She thought she could buy whatever she wanted—happiness, companionship, and love. She did find the best imitations of them, but they only distracted her from realizing that she really wanted genuine happiness, companionship, and love.

How had she lived like this for so long? Party after party, blur after blur. Lover after lover, fog after fog. And wine and wine and more wine.

Did anyone truly love her? And did she truly care for anyone but herself? She was frightened of the answer, too frightened to let it enter her mind.

Her brother was dead. A cardinal greatly honored and respected, yes, but to Orlean, this was nothing compared to his being her brother—her only brother. She hated the way they couldn't reconcile and how they felt like strangers. Over the years, Sabino had probably heard stories about the glamorous Lady Cavenaugh and her party yacht. It must have grieved him tremendously. She had been such a fool when he tried to be a brother and encouraged her in their only real conversation in fifty years. "How do you know there even is a God?" was all she could say to the brother she had hurt so much. He was trying to cheer her up with words he believed to be hope and truth. And all she could do was argue defensively. That was thoroughly selfish. Now he was dead.

A shadow swept over the ocean like a legion of phantom stingrays bound to roam through dark waters. Orlean held the flower in front of her like a candle in a cold temple—like a plea for understanding. All she needed was to be understood. If the gods had understood and been fair, they would not have given her cancer. But when have the gods been fair? Orlean had come to the conclusion of deities sometime during her loneliness when life seemed too hard to have evolved. No, there *were* gods, and they hated her. For cancer, loneliness, and sorrow are curses, and all curses have a sender. The gods had cursed her with a deceived, false life full of pretty things that distracted from the truth. That was cruel. The gods were cruel.

The bird of paradise flower rustled like a demure palm frond. Orlean saw her reflection wobble on the top of the Jacuzzi water. Why had she come out here to wait for death? Oh, that's right; it was because she had drowned her husband. Lord Cavenaugh had thought Orlean knew nothing of his adulterous affairs and went for a midnight swim. But Lady Cavenaugh *had* found out and planned revenge. He betrayed her so frivolously! He betrayed her barely two weeks after their wedding when he had promised her a blessed

forever. But soon he muttered the same words to
another girl between his depraved caresses! She had
passed the door and heard it, peeked in and seen it.
But she never let him know. He died oblivious. It was
simple, really. All she had to do was add electricity to
water. Death was very easy.

Now she had to die the same way. Orlean
concluded that this is how the gods work. They
punish you for your necessary sins; they load you
down with haunting guilt when you really don't feel
guilty. Then they leave you with loneliness and let
you drift and suffer, just so you will cry out to them.
Then they come back with the most irrevocable
punishment—death. Now she had to die. Oh, she
wished she hadn't done it! She wished someone else
had done it! Then she could have lived without blood
on her hands. Without the curses! She could have
kept her innocence and been felt sorry for; she could
have kept her honesty and been able to truly enjoy
the pleasures. That would have been justice. She
wished she had not killed her husband if only he had
died some other way.

But he didn't.

Connor was assigned to watch the chef's bedroom
door overnight, a rather boring job that
consisted of listening to the chef's muffled snores
through the wall and sitting on a hard floor. Connor

had fastened a large combination lock on the exterior of the door, which seemed fairly strong. He wasn't worried about the chef breaking out, which allowed Connor to migrate down the hallway. He was now intertwined with Shanlee on the leather sofa in the library on deck one. An aquamarine glow shone through the skylights in the bottom of the pool above, casting beautiful rippling shimmers onto the young couple. It was the only light in the library. With one hand, Connor pressed Shanlee closer to him. With the other hand, he caressed her precious fingers as they discussed the day.

"You were wonderful today," Shanlee whispered. "The way you captured the chef. You're so brave."

"Thank you. But I have to tell you something," said Connor.

"What's that?"

"I found another caterpillar. An orange one on the table."

Shanlee raised her head off his chest. "What? So the murderer might be someone else?"

"I don't know. Maybe the chef put it there before we caught him. It's possible, isn't it?"

"Oh, I hope you're right." She thought for a minute. "What if it's my uncle?"

"But what would he gain from the murders?"

"Maybe money?"

Connor nodded. "It's an idea. But wouldn't we hear him moving around the yacht? He's a big guy."

"He could have more stealth than we realize."

Connor wrapped both arms around her, hugging her tightly. "I hope it's the chef. That means you're safe." He kissed the top of her head.

Shanlee pulled away. "Con, I'm not ready to kiss."

He sighed. "Okay. That's fine."

"These nights with you have been phenomenal, a dream come true. But I'm still a simple homeschool girl from Nevada." She laughed. "You're the first boy I've ever dated."

Connor smiled. "I haven't even asked you to coffee yet. Are we really dating?"

Shanlee smacked him affectionately. "If these aren't dates I don't know what they are."

Connor wrapped both arms around her again. "I'm sorry. These are dates. We are together. It's just so secret and so fast. But I like it. I like you."

"I think I've told you all of my secrets," Shanlee whispered. "But there's something you're not telling me."

He scooted down the couch, leaving only one hand on her shoulder.

"Is it true, Connor? Is there something you're not telling me?"

He cleared his throat as quietly as he could. "I haven't told you what happened in my high school years."

"Well, I'm here and it's only two or three in the morning. We've got time."

Connor breathed a laugh. But then he sighed heavily. "I'm not ready, Shanlee. I don't want to talk about it right now."

Shanlee placed her head back on his chest as they drew close again. "That's okay. When do you think you'll be ready?"

He stroked her silky hair. But he didn't answer.

The unmistakable thump of footsteps sounded from the grand staircase. Connor jumped to his feet. "Come on. We have to check this out."

21

Tiptoeing as quietly as they could, Connor and Shanlee ascended the stone-inlaid steps. The dim glow of the LED backlight illuminated their way. The sound of footsteps guided them to deck three, and then they went muffled.

Grasping each other's hands as if their lives depended on it, Connor and Shanlee walked into the open doorway of the galley. There was Ronald Jennings riffling through the cabinets. He jolted at the sight of them. "You could have said something!" He narrowed his eyes at their hands. "Are you two a couple now? Young people. So impulsive." He bent over as he ransacked a cabinet.

Connor continued holding Shanlee's hand. "What are you doing?"

"I'm looking for the remote satellite device that I had in my suitcase. It's been missing since the captain was knocked off. The chef didn't want to die. He would have hidden it somewhere, probably in this kitchen." Ronald slammed the cabinet shut. "But I can't find anything!" And then his tone changed. He looked at Connor and Shanlee as if they were his employees. "You two, go wake up the others—except for Lady Cavenaugh. She's sick. She needs her rest."

"But it's three in the morning," said Shanlee.

Ronald scowled at her as if she was a disobedient child. "I said go wake up the others! I'm in charge now. Preston is off the throne. We found the killer. Now it's time to get back to America before we die here in the middle of the ocean. Wake up the others. Now!"

Everyone gathered on the cream-colored sofas and armchairs in the lounge on deck three. Ronald stood beside the shimmering grand piano. Connor and Shanlee decided to sit together, even if it worried Preston, but they didn't hold hands this time. Najah Hasan wrapped her black headscarf tightly around herself, her arms disappearing in the folds of her black dress. Tanya clenched a watery throw pillow, one hand on her stoic husband. Preston fixed a distrustful gaze on his brother. Durand's forehead was intensely creased under his curly locks; he did not look pleased about missing his shuteye. Clayton and Orlean weren't there.

"Where's the kid?" Ronald huffed.

"We decided to let him sleep," Preston answered. "He's only seven."

"Clay could sleep through anything," Tanya added. "He didn't even budge when Connor knocked on our door."

Ronald held up a flat palm in the direction of Tanya's face. "I get the picture." He raised his head like a CEO conducting a managerial meeting. "Now. We are stuck on a yacht in the middle of the Atlantic. That needs to change. Who wants to get back to the US as soon as possible?"

Everyone raised a hand.

"Okay. No boat or barge has stopped to help us because they have no indication that we are in need of help. If someone spotted us they wouldn't even stop! So, we have to find the distress flag and hang it high with a spotlight on it. Connor and you, the maid. What's your name again?"

"Najah," she answered curtly.

"All right. Connor and Najah. You two are the only crew on this yacht, who aren't locked up, that is. Do either of you know where the distress flag is kept? Surely you've been trained on this."

"It's kept in the captain's bridge," Najah replied. "But I looked for it yesterday and it wasn't there."

Ronald scowled. "Well, that isn't good enough, Najah! Keep looking for it until you find it! The chef wouldn't have destroyed the distress flag. I can guarantee that."

Najah looked at the floor.

The yacht seemed to rock more than usual as Ronald stomped to the other side of the lounge.

"Okay, everyone! I'm going to assign each of you a task to complete. And when you have completed it, report back to me.

"Najah, make us a lot of coffee." Ronald paused. "Actually no. I don't trust you. Tanya, you and Shanlee make us all coffee and breakfast. I'm sure you can find your way around the galley." He pointed a fat finger at Connor and Durand. "You, steward, show this teenager around the yacht, and while you do that, search for the distress flag and my remote satellite and the radio! You got that?"

"Yes, sir," said Connor.

Ronald faced his brother. "Preston, you get to come with me to the bridge. We're going to figure out how to captain a broken ship."

Preston nodded his consent.

Najah glanced from side to side. "What would you like me to do, sir?"

"You are going to stay here," Ronald commanded. "Play the piano. Polish the furniture. Vacuum the floor. I don't care. Just don't leave deck three. If you do, I will lock you up like we did to the chef. So you'd better behave."

Ronald thudded backward, making harsh eye contact with each person. "All right people, let's find our way back to America before we become a floating tomb!"

The motors whirred loudly in the white engine room as Connor and Durand searched the yacht. "I don't see anything from our list in here," said Connor. "At least we know the boat is still kind of working."

No response. It had been an awkward search so far. Durand wasn't much of a talker.

They exited the engine room.

"Let's check the cinema," said Connor as they walked across the hallway and opened the black door. The room contained several black leather armchairs, posters of 1960s films, a large screen, and dim lighting. "What kind of movies do you like, Durand?"

The teenager shrugged. "I like sci-fi and fantasy. I like movies with good swordfights."

Connor scanned the DVDs that took up the entire wall in the back of the room. "Well, you can certainly find a movie in here. Lady Cavenaugh has quite the collection, doesn't she?"

Durand smiled sheepishly. "Yeah, I could, huh? Maybe we can watch a movie in here after we're done searching? Will you watch a movie with me?"

"It's a thought," said Connor dubiously. "But I don't know what the new captain Ronald would say."

Durand wiped his nose and blinked, as if disappointed.

"Let's see what we accomplish. If we find the flag, maybe we can find some time for a movie. Okay?"

Durand hung his head, burying his hands in his baggy pockets. "Okay. If you say so."

Tanya and Shanlee poured eight cups of foamy cappuccinos into eight Italian mugs. And then Preston entered. The part in his graying hair was out of alignment, maybe for the first time in his life.

"How's it going?" Tanya asked worriedly.

Preston grimaced. "We're still working on the boat. There's a great deal of damage. However,"—he raised an orange cloth—"we found the distress flag."

"Wonderful!" The women clapped their hands together ecstatically.

Preston turned to his adopted daughter. "Can you please do a favor for me?"

Shanlee rushed up to him. "Yes! Absolutely!"

"Go up to the stern of deck four. There you will find a flagpole that is currently holding a flag with the Cavenaugh family crest. Please replace it with the distress flag."

"Yes, sir! I will do that, Dad!" Giving him a quick hug, she rushed out the door.

The hints of morning light were just beginning to show on the horizon as Shanlee strode to the back of deck four. She was feeling hopeful. They had found the distress flag and caught the chef. And they were trying to figure out how to get the yacht moving again. But mostly, she was thrilled about her budding romance with Connor. Last night they had almost kissed. How exciting! She wanted to tell her parents.

Today, she would have to talk with Connor about that. Her cheeks warmed with affection despite the bitter wind.

After she replaced the flag and mounted the pole securely into its holder, she watched it struggle and fight—an orange sheet with a black square and a circle.

Before she went downstairs, Shanlee wanted to check out the sun deck. Maybe there was a hidden storage container up there. She climbed the exterior staircase, gliding her arm on the slippery railing.

And then she saw the body.

22

The Past

Connor was sixteen. He had just returned to Nevada after spending five months at a military boarding school out of state. His first objective was to get back into JROTC. Blake Stonewell was still attending JROTC meetings, climbing the ranks and sitting with the senior guys in the front of the classroom. Unfortunately, whenever he passed Connor in the hallway, he turned the other way, as if Connor did not exist. When Connor walked up to a group of guys, Blake would step away from the circle after a few seconds. Blake never allowed himself to be near Connor for long.

This brought a particular level of misery to Connor. He missed his old friend. Putting on this façade that everything was okay at JROTC, when Blake was clearly avoiding his gaze at all costs, was like a sharp pricking of his heart again and again and again. Would he one day grow numb to this? Connor wished he had never sent those stupid emails. He wanted to explain to Blake what happened.

One afternoon, Connor dialed up his friend Logan Castlehall with a special request. "Hey, Logan, would you mind if I logged in to your social media account? The Stonewells blocked my account and my phone number. I just want to look at Blake's page and see how he's been doing."

"That's an idea. I guess I could give you my password. You haven't been able to catch up with Blake at JROTC?"

"No!" Connor lamented. "He won't even look at me and he walks away whenever I'm around."

"That's rough, Con. I'm sorry. My password is 'twouble' with a 'W.' All lowercase."

"Thanks, Logan. You're the best."

That night, Connor rolled up on the swivel chair at the computer desk in the living room, fingers eager to type Logan's password: *t-w-o-u-b-l-e*.

He was in.

Immediately, Connor went to Blake's page and pressed the message button. He was impersonating Logan. Blake responded right away.

Blake: Oh hey Logan! How's it going?

Logan/Connor: Not bad. I just wanted to talk with you about something.

Blake: Okay, go ahead. I'm ready lol

Logan/Connor: Haha cool. So at JROTC, it seems like you haven't been talking with Connor anymore. You guys used to be good friends. Is there something going on?

Blake: Sorry, I can't tell you about that.

Frustrated that he was getting nowhere, Connor tried a more direct approach.

Logan/Connor: Hey Blake, it's me Connor. I got Logan's password. I just wanted to tell you that this isn't right! The friendship between our families all fell apart because of the emails I sent you last year. I believe there is a way to resolve this! A way to make it right. Can we meet to talk about it?

There was no response.

Of course, Logan's parents were called and then Connor's parents.

A week later, the freckled face and the sharp buzz cut of Logan Castlehall pulled up into the Alekseevs' driveway. Connor hopped into the passenger seat, ready to carpool to JROTC on the other side of town.

"I'm sorry for impersonating you, Logan. I shouldn't have done that," said Connor as they drove down the dusty road.

"It's okay, Con. I understand. Seems like the Stonewells' rejection has been hard on you."

Connor shook his head. "You have no idea."

"Oh, but I should to tell you, my mom doesn't want us to hang out anymore."

"What?" said Connor, surprised. "Because of the social media thing?"

"Partially. She spoke with Mrs. Stonewell on the phone for a long time. After that she was pretty upset. My mom thinks you're going to be a bad influence on me."

"Oh come on, now you guys are rejecting me too?" said Connor. "What is happening to my life?"

"I'm not, Con. I don't agree with her at all. I think we should still be friends. Maybe I can convince her to let me drive you to JROTC meetings. She probably won't let me visit your house anymore, though."

Connor and Logan entered the boxy military building where JROTC meetings took place. Framed black-and-white photographs hung on the walls, featuring tanks on beaches and men jumping out of airplanes. Connor and Logan started greeting their buddies.

A stocky woman emerged, wearing a camouflage uniform from head to toe. "Alekseev, come with me."

"Oh boy," teased one of Connor's friends, nicknamed Frenchie. "The colonel wants you."

"I'd better hurry, then," said Connor with a laugh. He followed Colonel Highridge to a back room. Something must be up. She was usually a bit friendly, even when she was firm. But she was so grave now.

Colonel Highridge closed the door and stood in front of him. Her face was square like a brick. "Alekseev, this week I received a report from Cadet Major Stonewell's parents that you impersonated another member of the group over social media. Is this true?"

"Yes, but I already apologized to Logan about it."

"It's not just that," Colonel Highridge continued. "Last week, during a game of ultimate frisbee, the Stonewells said that you accused him of following you around. Is this true?"

"I mean, yeah, I was mad. It was just a crazy thing that you say when you're upset." Connor sighed. "What's going on, Colonel? Why are you talking with me about this?"

She held up her finger. "They also said that you attempted to contact Blake by leaving him a note, with a twenty-dollar-bill, in his binder. Is this true?"

Connor's heartbeat escalated. "Yes, it was a birthday card."

She clenched her strong jaw, her face becoming even more square. "The Stonewells said that you were instructed to never contact them again. Did they not make this request clear to you?"

Connor sighed heavily. "No, they-they made it clear." He lifted his face. "But you don't understand! Our families used to be close. Blake used to be one of my best friends! We used to have gatherings every summer at my parents' house when the Greenwoods and the Stonewells all came over and we made a full day of it. And that was all ruined because of a couple stupid emails I sent about a year or so ago! I've been trying to explain to them that it's all been a big misunderstanding. I was dealing with some dark thoughts that I was trying to figure out, so I trusted Blake and his mom with this. But then they turned on me and…"

Colonel Highridge shook her head gravely. "I can't help you figure out how to get your families to be friends again, Alekseev. Regardless, it appears that the Stonewells made it very clear to you that they do not want you to contact them anymore. But ever since you returned to our battalion, you made repeated efforts to contact Cadet Major Stonewell, like you just admitted in your own words."

"Yeah, it's so aggravating!" said Connor, throwing out his arms. "They won't let me explain that it was all one big, horrible misunderstanding! They refuse to listen to anything I have to say!"

Colonel Highridge narrowed her brow. "Words have power, Connor Alekseev. You can't just erase what you've said."

Connor fell silent.

"Blake is one of our most valuable leaders," the Colonel went on. "He has a real shot at getting into the military. But your being here is making that more difficult." A crack appeared in her stern armor.

"There is another JROTC program across town that you could join."

"Oh, I don't want to go anywhere else," said Connor. "This is where all my friends go. Skander and Gael Greenwood just started attending last week. I want to stay here."

Colonel Highridge put her hands behind her back, standing at parade rest. "I'm sorry, but that's not possible. Please turn in your uniforms and equipment to my office next week. You can never return to our battalion."

23

Connor, Durand, Ronald, Shanlee, Preston, and Tanya gathered into a shocked circle on the open-air sun deck at the top of the yacht. Ronald exhaled as a cold gust stole the smoke away from his Cuban cigar like famished sharks devouring a trickle of blood. Ronald stood still for a long moment and gave the cigar to the ocean.

Orlean Cavenaugh's body lay motionless, her face in the mirky water of the Jacuzzi, a hand hanging over the edge in an awkward position. Blood was still seeping out of the bullet hole in her head. Attached to the fingers of the dangling left hand by a hair clip was a white page and an orange origami butterfly, flapping in the wind. Ronald tore away the page, reading quickly. He handed the page to Preston, who read the handwritten poem aloud.

"Paradise,
Leave her to count the curses.
Euphoria,
Allow the crumpled maiden a try.

"Water Palace,
Can't you give her peace?
Pleasure Island,
What happened to promises?

"Beauty,
You've gone, vanished.
Goddess,
How could age defeat you?

"Know,
Reality conquers, kills.
Too much for you?
Fly away, little girl.
—The Glass Shadow"

For a moment no one spoke in the cold wind.

"This was never supposed to happen." Ronald shook his head. "Now we're all going to die." His small eyes were slightly tender despite the heavy frown.

Connor sighed. "I wish we had never gone on this cruise. I wish we were all living our lives back on land, as we should have. This was a huge mistake."

"You might be next," Ronald said bluntly. "Unless we catch this killer you might die."

"I know."

"Doesn't that bother you, boy?"

"Yes, extremely."

"You don't look like you're bothered."

"I am. Without a doubt." Connor's eyes were wide in bewilderment. He surveyed the troubled faces of Preston, Tanya and Shanlee. "I'm going to do whatever I can to discover who the killer is."

Ronald didn't look convinced. "Then go find the killer and tell me who it is."

"Okay."

Ronald stared suspiciously as they headed back inside.

A copy of the Constitution of the United States hung on the wall of the captain's stateroom in various separate frames. A few amendments were clearer than others. A two-dollar bill rested beneath the document in the final frame, displaying the picture of the Founding Fathers signing something.

Connor looked around the dead captain's room. He was trying to do whatever he could to discover clues, but he didn't understand anything. Nothing made sense. Who was the murderer already! Why did he or she leave butterflies and poems beside each body?

Connor left the room quietly and closed the door behind him. He heard an argument coming from Ronald's room. He stopped and listened.

"I am doing the best I can. My investigation is almost complete. Just give me a little more time—"

"A little more time! Preston, you fool! Now Orlean is gone, and you are asking for time? Don't you see that at any moment another one of us could be killed?"

"Ronald, please…"

"You have until noon, Preston. If you don't find out the murderer's identity by then, I will get rid of the person that I most suspect."

Preston opened the door and saw Connor. Ronald glared at him hatefully.

"Come with me, Connor." Preston motioned for him to follow, stooping over and moving slowly as if he were elderly rather than middle-aged. He seemed thinner. "I saw you looking around." They stopped in front of Preston's room.

"Yeah. I was trying to find some evidence," said Connor.

"Did you?"

"No. Not yet."

"I could use your help with something, if you're willing."

"What's that?"

"Could you stay in my stateroom with my wife and my children while I continue my investigation? I would greatly appreciate it."

"You don't suspect me of anything? I think your brother does."

"No. I don't suspect you. I don't completely trust you either but I trust you enough." Preston opened the door. Shanlee and Tanya were in the room, talking softly. Clayton was playing with action figure toys on the carpet floor. Durand was sprawled out on the bed, reading his fantasy novel once again. Connor walked in as Preston headed off.

Tanya nodded to Connor but didn't speak. She closed her eyes and began praying silently. He decided not to disturb her.

Shanlee sat on the loveseat with a Bible opened on her lap. Connor joined her. He tried to comfort her by smiling weakly. "Hi."

"Hello, Connor." She spoke with deep care mingled with concern. "What have you been doing?"

"Oh, just looking around. Not getting anything done, though."

"Do you have any suspicions?" she whispered.

"Some, but I don't know anymore. How about you?"

"I—I hate to say." She glanced toward her mom. "I snuck into the cardinal's room earlier to see the butterfly and poem that all of you saw last night. Mom was telling me about it. I—" She paused and collected her thoughts. "It looked like it was folded out of a pink church bulletin. There was something very familiar about it."

"What?"

"I unfolded it and found out that it came from a church back in Henderson. I have a few friends who used to go there. But that's not even it. Two names were written on the back in the section entitled

'Special Guests,' " she whispered very softly. "Cardinal Sabino Verdone and *Ronald Jennings*."

Connor thought rapidly. "So, your uncle knew the cardinal?"

"It certainly seems that way." Shanlee leaned closer to him. "Like I was saying last night, I think my uncle is the murderer. He never visited us before and hasn't said a word to me the whole trip. He's been unfair to my dad. I think he hates us."

"He was acting a little strange this morning," said Connor, "when he had us wake up everyone in the yacht, except for Lady Cavenaugh."

Shanlee sighed. "I don't want to believe that he did it. I can't believe that any of us would do something so terrible."

Connor saw the pain in her moist brown eyes. He wanted to glide his fingers through her silky black hair, but he resisted.

"How are you, Shanlee? Deep down, how are you handling all this death around us?"

She seemed grateful that he asked. "I can't understand *why* it's happening! My dad accepted this trip only a short time ago and now all this. I don't know what to think."

"Yeah. I know what you mean." Connor rubbed his chin.

Durand rose to his feet. "Hey, I'm going to go down to the deck one library. It's quieter there."

Tanya blinked rapidly. "Oh. Okay. But come right back."

"I will," said the teenager as he exited through the stateroom door.

Connor and Shanlee glanced at each other.

Durand O'Reilly wished he had changed his name to Jennings as he sat alone in the deck one library, trying to read his novel. He had made such a big deal out of keeping the last name he was born with. "It would be betrayal," he had said to Tanya.

"I can understand that, Durand. You have every right in the world to keep your last name." Those past encouraging words of hers didn't hold him to his decision any more. Changing his name could have made him a different person. It could have helped him forget.

Durand shook his head, trying to shake out the returning haunt. Today was horrible. The reading of his book was only bringing back the haunt, not drowning it like it should. Every other minute, he was back out in the night, scraped by the black asphalt, watching his house burn, his parents inside, and hearing his mother's scream. His mother's scream. That was living death if ever there was. How could he get it out of his head? He could handle the flames devouring his house; he could handle half his life lost in it but not his mother's scream. Maybe if he had only changed his name and become a completely different person, he could live freely. Nothing seemed to drive the scream out. The scream, the scream, the scream...

Durand put down the book, stood, and eyed the bookcase behind him, scanning the titles. Maybe another book could drown the haunt. He found *On the Origin of Species* by Charles Darwin. Yes, that was perfect. *There's nothing like science as an escape from life,* he thought.

"Hello, Durand."

Startled, Durand looked up and saw Preston Jennings.

"Hello, Preston," he said flatly.

"Interesting read you're holding," Preston commented.

"Yes, it is."

Preston glanced at the coffee table, bent down, and began turning a book toward his view. "Has anyone else been down here today?"

"Yes. The maid a few times."

"You should call her Ms. Hasan. It's more respectful."

"Oh. Okay."

Preston stared down at the table again and lifted up a book. "Did you see who was looking at this?" The book cover had a black-and-white picture of Japanese calligraphy and a stone.

"I'm not sure. I know Ms. Hasan was looking through most of the shelves." He pointed to the farthest shelf. "But she was very quiet."

The face of Preston Jennings showed his discomfort. There was a new touch of sadness among his blurring gray eyes.

"Thank you, Durand. We will probably have a meeting soon. I will see you there."

Preston slowly made his way up to deck three and to the dinner table. There in the center of the polished wood were two caterpillars; one was a deep-maroon color, and the other was folded from a dollar bill. They were pointed away from each other, toward opposite ends, bending as if they were each inching away. Two more were threatened with death, and Preston was supposed to stop it.

With heavy, dragging steps, he trudged down to his stateroom and entered. The room was silent as Connor and Shanlee rose to greet Preston. Clayton dropped his toys and ran to embrace him. Tanya turned from gazing out the window. Preston met the four concerned looks with his own and fell into the armchair.

"Preston!" Tanya ran to him and knelt at his side. "Oh, Preston, what are we going to do? How are we going to get out of this… No one has come. There isn't a boat or a plane or anything to signal to. Have you found out who it is? Do you know?"

"I have a strong inclination to believe it is a certain individual."

Connor listened eagerly.

"*Who*, my darling?"

Preston gazed into his wife's eyes. "I can't tell you yet, my Tanya. I have to find more solid evidence first. We need to pray now, for all of us but especially for the murderer. That is the best thing we can do."

Shanlee and Connor exchanged glances as Preston began to pray in a low tone while Mrs. Jennings sobbed beside him.

24

"Where is Najah?" Ronald asked with a frown carved so deeply into his features one would wonder if he had ever smiled. "I told her to stay in this room! She defied my orders."

Connor and Clayton took their seats in the lounge on deck three.

"Shanlee is getting her now." Tanya Jennings attempted a smile, but her worry drowned it.

Connor stood even though he had just sat down. "What? Where did she go?"

"That way. Down the hall." Tanya was startled by Connor's sudden concern. "Ms. Hasan was giving Lady Cavenaugh's room a final cleaning."

Connor didn't like it. "I think I'll go see what's keeping them."

"Oh no you don't," Ronald growled. "You are staying right here while we wait for Preston."

Connor could see suspicion clearly in Ronald's glaring eyes. "Seriously, Mr. Jennings, I think I should check on the women."

"No!" Ronald shouted, more angrily. "You are staying right here where I can watch you."

"Are you implying, sir, that you believe me to be the murderer?"

"You do look like you could stab someone with a knife."

Tanya gasped.

"Mr. Jennings, I have never killed anyone in my life."

Ronald's face was getting quite red. "Only another fool like you would believe that. You might be able to deceive the others but not me. You're a killer. I know it."

"I am not." Connor spoke the words very clearly as if to make sure Ronald heard. Ronald merely glared with even more hatred. Connor focused, preparing himself; he watched the other's hands to make sure they weren't finding a gun in his jacket. Ronald's hand was in his left pocket.

"I wonder what's taking my husband so long." Tanya broke the tension, saying her desperately worried thought more out of overwhelmed concern than to prevent a fight.

A sudden, all-too-possible suspicion grew wildly in Ronald's mind. He lurched toward the grand staircase. "Come with me!"

Thinking the same thing, Connor and Tanya glanced at each other and followed with Clayton right behind them.

Security, Tanya's precious security, began to die as if trampled by the wild thump of footsteps. *It can't be, it can't be* was all she could think.

Ronald was bending over the body when Connor, Clay, and Tanya entered the stateroom on deck two. With his back facing them, Ronald removed his hands from the neck and stood straight. *It can't be, it can't be* raced again through Tanya's mind as her breathing refused to slow. *Please, Preston darling, wake up. It's your Tanya, your Tanya!* She almost expected him to get up off the floor—regardless of the blood that was draining out of the round hole in his chest— and say, as if nothing had happened, "Hello, my darling." *Just say it, love. Just say it.*

Clayton's jaw dropped as he stepped closer. Connor reached out and picked him up. "No, Clay. Stay with me."

Holding a white sheet of paper and the butterfly in his right hand, Ronald Jennings turned around. The three looked up at him as if to find a sign refuting what they already knew. Without returning their looks, Ronald walked forward, handed the poem and butterfly to Mrs. Jennings, and left.

Devastation and reality began to sink into Tanya's heart like a chainless anchor that was sinking deeper and deeper into the watery depths as she saw the origami butterfly folded from a twenty-dollar bill and read the poem:

Give me! Give me!
Look, it's shiny.
Give me, give me,
See, it's gold.

Hand me, hand me,
My palms are ready,
Hand me, hand me,
The gems are mine.

Paper kingdom,
Let me have it.
Green back power,
Grant me more.

I will hold you,
keep you, know you.
I will hoard you,
All is mine.
—The Glass Shadow

A heavy earthen pot rested beneath a spotlight in the corner of the deck one library, maroon glaze dripping down the rim in stilled adornment. Tanya Elizabeth Jennings sat alone, staring at the decorative vessel beneath the spotlight. Some sunlight leaked in through the skylight under the pool above, dancing around on the carpet before her. Her heart was ripped and torn but somehow still beating. She uttered the same prayer over and over, "Lord, I want to be with you. Please help me. Please protect my children." Now that she was free of her guilt, her prayers were more peaceful. It was as though God was in the room.

Shanlee hurried down the stairs. "Mom?"

No answer. Connor followed with Clayton at his side.

"She must be in the library! Where else could she be? Mom?" Shanlee stood at the bottom step and entered the room. There was her mother sitting in the farthest seat, looking calmly toward her. "Oh, Mom!" Shanlee raced over and hugged her as Connor watched. "Are you all right?"

Clayton snuggled up beside Tanya on the sofa. "Are you very sad, Mommy?"

"I don't think it's settled in yet." Mrs. Jennings had a dazed expression that Connor knew would worry Shanlee.

"It's okay. I'm here. I'm here!" Shanlee began to weep while she maintained her embrace. "We can do this; we just have to stay together through the rest of it."

Tanya patted her daughter's shoulder. "It will be okay. But there's something I need to tell you."

Shanlee dabbed her cheeks. "All right. What's that?"

"It's something I was going to tell your father, actually. But I'll go ahead and tell you instead." Tanya pulled Clayton close to herself, hoping he wouldn't understand. "When I was a teenager, I fell in love and got pregnant. But the thing is, I-I didn't keep the baby. I went to a clinic."

A bundle of emotions was caught in Shanlee's face—confusion, acceptance, and sorrow.

"I never told anyone else about it until the other evening, when I went to confession with Mr. Verdone." Tanya smiled. "I'm not Catholic, but I really needed that. He pronounced forgiveness over me and for some reason, this time, it sank in. It worked. Now I feel clean. Different. New. I finally feel this truth deep within me: it is the blood of Jesus Christ that washes away sin, not the sweat and tears of Tanya Jennings."

"That's wonderful!" said Shanlee.

"It is, yes." Tanya smiled peacefully and then sighed. "But I was planning on telling Preston. He was such a workaholic, you know. We weren't as close as I would have liked. I thought there was still time to fix that. But now…."

Tanya lifted Clayton off her lap. "Why don't you go off with Connor?" She looked right at her daughter's eyes, firm and true. "You too."

"What?" Shanlee recoiled. "No! I'm going to stay with you."

"Actually, I'd like to be alone for a little while. Please."

Shanlee's brow scrunched into a knot. "What?"

"Please, my dearest daughter. Thank you for hearing me out and for being so kind. But I need to be alone for a little while."

Shanlee's eyes were full of compassion. "Okay. I understand."

At the base of the stairs, Ronald glared at Connor, then down the hall at the women with a cold scowl on his face. There was a complete stillness in the room as Tanya and Shanlee noticed him. Shanlee gave her mother a final hug, got up, and walked over to Ronald. "Yes?" she asked in a whisper. He didn't answer. "Please leave her alone, Uncle Ronald. She wants to be by herself."

Ronald blinked at Shanlee as a tear trickled down from one of his eyes. "Don't call me that."

Shanlee broke into tears and ran up the stairs. Connor stayed for a minute.

Ronald stared for too long at his sister-in-law. She was very demure, quiet, and still. "Who's the murderer?"

"I don't know," she replied.

"Didn't Preston tell you?"

"No."

Ronald shoved past Connor and left.

Connor stopped beside Tanya. "Are you sure you want to be alone? It would be better if we stuck together."

"Um, Connor, I just lost my husband. Please. I need a few minutes."

Connor gave in. "All right. Come on, Clay. Let's see where your sister went."

Tanya was relieved. Peace, finally. Wonderful peace. Even though she was by herself in a room, she was not alone. It was as though she were paddling a row boat on a lake that was still as glass, and right before her rose a magnificent castle. There was a staircase that led down to the lake and people were standing on it. They were waving at Tanya. Her grandparents would be there, oh so happy to see her. Preston would be there, eager to wrap her in a tender hug. And her Savior would be there. The Lord Jesus, her true love. Tanya felt a little nervous to meet her Savior. But she was much less nervous than before.

Tanya felt like she had on the day of her wedding, when she prepared for the ceremony in the back room of that old brick church with the white steeple. Her bridesmaids were with her. They were all so spontaneous and giddy that day. They crafted flowery crowns and attempted to learn traditional Jewish dances. What goofballs. Even Tanya's mother had joined in. Oh, but it had been good. So good. Somehow, today was like that.

Warm tears swelled in her eyes.

And then she heard footsteps. She looked up and gasped.

25

Ronald Jennings pounded his angry fist on the door of the master's suite on deck three as Connor emerged from the grand staircase. Shanlee and Clayton were standing there watching.

"What are you doing?" Connor asked.

Ronald glared at him with a murderous rage. "The maid has locked herself into Orlean's bedroom!" He pounded harder than ever, shaking the floor, but the door did not budge. Ronald tromped over to the staircase, ascending the steps as he muttered to himself, "Oh no she did not!"

Connor huddled together with Shanlee and Clay. "All right. We have to go get your mother. Things are heating up." As they scrambled down the stairs, Connor said, "Let's go to Brock's room. I have something there that we might need."

"What's that?" Shanlee questioned as they rushed down the hallway of staterooms, entering the chief officer's room, which Connor had been using. He strode over to his suitcase beneath the porthole in the wood-paneled wall. In a hidden compartment,

Connor retrieved a package. And in that package was a six-shooter revolver.

"Whoa! You have a gun?" said Clayton, pointing.

"Yes. But it's just for me to use, buddy." Connor turned to Shanlee, pointing the revolver at the floor.

"What are we going to do?" she asked.

"You guys stay here and lock the door," said Connor. "I'll go get your mother."

"Bring Durand too," said Shanlee.

"Right. Yes. I'll look for him too." Before he walked out, Connor checked the closets. "Hey, please search this room while I'm gone. Who knows what else is in here."

Connor's mind raced along with his feet. There were only three possible options remaining: the Najah, Ronald, or Durand. Connor refused to suspect Tanya or Shanlee. He couldn't believe that murder would be in their characters.

As Connor entered the library on deck one, he saw Tanya Jennings's body lying on the glass-bottom floor. There was a little blood around the red circle in her shoulder. Connor knelt down and checked her pulse. She was dead.

Connor dropped to the ground as he picked up the poem and the maroon paper butterfly.

Come, enter,
Great to see you!
How was life?

Come, sit,
I'll go tell him.
Don't be afraid to touch.

Come, with me,
He's ecstatic,
Cannot wait.

Come, follow,
His name?
We call him Reaper.

Come, be excited,
He will love you,
He will smile at you.

Come, here we are,
Enter slowly,
No, there's nothing to fear.

Come—

Connor cast the page aside, deciding not to finish it.

This was a huge blow. Tanya was a wonderful woman who reminded Connor of the kindhearted matrons from his childhood. Tanya was like them, a woman led by strong ideals and complete dedication to her family. How would he tell Shanlee?

Connor sighed heavily. He noticed a stack of books on the coffee table. The one on the bottom read *The Sword in the Opal Sea*. Connor reached over and pulled out the book. On the cover were animated warriors, colorful monsters, and roaring waves in the background. It looked like many other typical fantasy novels. He opened the book, but something was wrong with the pages. The back half didn't bend properly. Flipping to the spot, Connor discovered that the back pages were glued together. He went to the topmost page of that section and tore through it.

There was the remote satellite.

The realization swept over Connor. Quickly he dropped the satellite into his pocket and raced up the stairs.

26

The Past

Seventeen-year-old Connor strode down the hallways of Green Valley Fitness Center. He had started attending because they had a well-equipped room where he could practice his martial arts—with quality punching bags, floor mats, and plenty of space. The squeaking of shoes on a basketball court filled the air, accompanied by a dim rubbery smell. As he passed the courts, Diego Stonewell walked out in shorts and a sleeveless jersey. "Connor!" he exclaimed. "Great to see you!"

"Hey, Diego." Connor was surprised by the exuberant greeting. Diego was treating him like an old friend. Did he not know that his parents and Blake had shunned Connor? He was probably oblivious. "Since when have you been coming here?"

"Oh, my family and I have been working out at this gym for ages," Diego answered. "My mom comes here almost every morning." He pointed a goofy finger at Connor. "Dude, I miss boffer wars in your backyard."

"Me too, man," said Connor. "Now we have to be grown-ups or something." Connor waved farewell and went about his day.

So, Mrs. Stonewell came to this same gym? What a small world. Connor had a bright idea. He would go to the gym at the same time as Mrs. Stonewell and plead his case with her. He could finally explain, in person, that it had all been one big, horrible misunderstanding. Then they could finally reconcile! The Stonewells and the Greenwoods would come back to the Alekseevs' house. Connor and all the kids would hang out and play games in the backyard while the moms chattered away in the butterfly garden. Overtime, somehow, Blake would warm up to Connor and they would be like brothers again. The precious memories of his childhood would be restored at last. Yes! This would surely help!

A few days later, when Connor arrived at Green Valley Fitness Center, he noticed the Stonewells' big gray SUV in the parking lot. She was here! Mrs. Stonewell was here! Quickly Connor stowed his bag in the locker room and roamed around the gym.

There, across the room on an exercise bike, was Mrs. Stonewell, conversing with some other lady. Connor was a little nervous. What if she didn't want to speak with him? He decided he would have to try anyway. Mrs. Stonewell had once been a close friend and confidante, one of Connor's two most trusted people in the world. Surely such a wonderful woman like her would at least listen to him.

Slowly Connor walked up to the exercise bikes and climbed onto the one right beside Mrs. Stonewell's.

"Mrs. Stonewell, hi!"

Her eyes widened as she looked at him. "Oh! Hi, how are you?"

"I'm good, I just wanted to…"

But Mrs. Stonewell had turned back to the other lady.

"Mrs. Stonewell, Andalucía, I need to talk with you. It's important."

She didn't look at him again. All Connor could see was the wavy black hair with auburn highlights on the back of her head.

And then he realized the truth. Mrs. Stonewell was ignoring him. She didn't want to talk with him at all.

Quietly Connor slid off the exercise bike and fled the gym as fast as he could.

The next day Mr. Alekseev walked up to Connor, shaking his head in annoyance. "I just got an email from Norman Stonewell. He doesn't want you to go to Green Valley Fitness Center before 11 a.m. He says it bothers his wife."

Connor felt sick to his stomach.

"But you know what, Con? I disagree!" Mr. Alekseev declared. "You can go there if you want. Work out! Practice your karate. Do your thing. Forget the Stonewells! This isn't fair to you." He walked away mumbling to himself. "Psh, Norman. Who does he think he is? Telling my son where to go and where not to go…"

Connor was very grateful for how his dad stood up for him. But Connor was not feeling well. He didn't want to return to Green Valley Fitness Center ever again.

The following week, Connor searched the crowd at the conference for the Nevada Society of Homeschool Families. People from all over the state were trickling in through the big glass doors. Young families pushed strollers and held the hands of little toddlers. Large families with eight or more children marched into the building like a clan meeting at an ancient gathering place. Well-dressed grandparents squabbled with each other about being late as they hurried ahead for the doors to the auditorium. It was the night of the graduation ceremony.

Connor walked up to a brawny man in an expensive suit, Norman Stonewell. "Sir, I wanted to tell you that I mean no ill at all toward you and your family."

"I know that, Connor."

"Then why do you treat me like you do? I really respect Blake. I think it would be great if our families could be friends again."

Norman adjusted the collar of his fine shirt. "No. We cannot fellowship with you because it wouldn't be right."

Blake walked up and began listening in.

"Why wouldn't it be right?" Connor asked Norman. "Why?"

"Because it would be unhealthy," Norman answered.

Blake interjected. "Connor, I don't want to be your friend anymore. It's not just my parents. Okay? Please leave us alone."

Connor reeled backward. For years, he had trusted Blake more than his other friends. Before the rejection, Blake had always treated Connor with a steady, brotherly love—with smiles, firm handshakes, words of respect, and listening ears. Connor had assumed that it was Mr. Stonewell who had insisted on pulling the friendship apart; he had assumed that Blake still wanted to be friends but was just trying to respect his father. But now, there was no more compassion behind the amber eyes.

Norman patted his son on the shoulder. "Why don't you go into the auditorium and find your mother? I'll be there soon."

Blake joined the flood of people entering the auditorium where the graduation ceremony was about to take place.

Norman held back. "What are friends, Connor?"

"Friends are people we care about," Connor replied. His face was suddenly feeling unusually cold.

"No. That's too simple." Norman fastened the top button of his blazer. "Friends are mutual influencers. You said that you respect my son. Great. Thank you. But there's a problem with this equation. You would influence my son too. And you are a distortion. You're a threat to the safety of my family. Why would I allow someone like you to build a friendship with my son?"

"Mr. Stonewell, I'm not actively pursuing wrongdoing! I'm trying to break free of it."

Norman chuckled dryly. "We can't help you with that. Now, I want to make one thing quite clear." He faced Connor squarely. "Never contact my family again. Do not speak with Blake, or any of my children, or my wife. Or I will bring this to the proper authorities. Do you understand me?"

Connor managed a small nod and walked away. There was no point in talking any longer. But he could feel Mr. Stonewell's eyes on the back of his neck. Connor hobbled over to a pillar, slid to the floor, and wept.

"Whoa! Whoa! What's wrong?" said the voice of Logan Castlehall as he knelt and placed a hand of comfort on Connor's shoulder.

But Connor couldn't reply. He was still weeping.

Logan moved on, entering the auditorium.

Connor was overwhelmed. The woman who was once like a second mom, who once brought food to Connor's family when they were in need, who used to be someone Connor could call when times were tough—she had requested that Connor never again visit the gym she went to in the mornings. And the man who was once like a big brother, who Connor had trusted more than anyone else with a scary secret, who had taken Connor under his wing like a true friend—he had told Connor to his face that he had no interest in being friends. And the father who guided them both had threatened to call the police if Connor ever contacted them again. What happened? The people who once smiled at the sight of Connor and gave him thoughtful, personalized gifts on his birthdays now wielded threats of legal action if he tried to speak with them anymore. Connor used to be a special boy with a bright future. Now he was lost.

For some reason, Connor still respected Blake and his mother. He still regarded them with high esteem. Years ago, he had made an unconscious pact of loyalty to them, a pact that was not easily broken. But that was the problem. That's why he was stuck.

Connor's nose filled with so much mucus that he had to seek out a solution. With a great effort, he rose from the ground and retrieved a paper towel from the bathroom. He pulled himself together and went into the auditorium, finding a seat next to a group of friends from his martial arts class.

Connor's heart pounded relentlessly as he attempted to listen to the graduation ceremony. But the wheels were turning in his mind. He could never be friends with the Stonewells again. Blake said himself that he wanted Connor to leave them alone. What was he to do? What was the next step? To be near was to be in pain. To live in the same community, to roam around in the same city, was to live with the possibility of encountering a Stonewell. The public shunning had rattled Connor to his core.

I can't live here anymore, Connor thought. *I have to leave.*

27

Shanlee pulled her hair as she collapsed onto the bed after receiving the news. "My mother is dead! And Durand is the murderer? How could this happen?"

"The remote satellite was in his book," said Connor. "It has to be him. Has Durand shown any indication of unusual behavior since he came into your home?"

"No. He's just been reclusive. He keeps to himself all the time, but a lot of kids do that." Shanlee thought for a minute. "Wait. There was one time when he took our old bloodhound on a walk. When he came back, he said that he lost the dog. We never found him." Shanlee looked at Connor doubtfully. "I don't think that's enough evidence."

"No. But this is evidence! The remote satellite was hidden in his book and I have it here now."

Shanlee jumped to her feet. "Okay. Then we need to call for help!"

"You're right." Connor removed his cell phone and tried to connect the remote satellite. It worked. Immediately he dialed 911.

"Massachusetts Coast Guard. What is your emergency?" said a man's voice on the other end.

Shanlee and Connor held hands victoriously. They had contacted someone!

"Hello, my name is Connor Alekseev. I'm on a yacht called the *Chrysalis*. We're stranded in the middle of the ocean. We need help."

"Roger. Can you share your exact location, please?"

"I'm not sure how to do that. We are using a remote satellite device."

"Roger. There should be a button on the back that says 'share location.'"

Sure enough. There it was. Connor clicked the button.

"One minute, sir."

There was a long, tense pause. Connor and Shanlee paced the room. Clayton pressed his face against the sliding glass door to the balcony, gazing at the ocean as if in a trance.

"The closest vessel is fifteen to twenty hours away. We can redirect their course to your location."

"Fifteen to twenty hours?" Shanlee shook her head rapidly. "Who knows what will happen on this ship in that time! That's too long."

"Sir," said Connor into his phone. "We are in a state of emergency. Six people are dead. There is a killer on board. We need assistance as soon as possible."

"Roger." There was another long pause. *"We will send out a rescue team in a chopper. It should arrive in five to six hours."*

"Thank you very much. That's perfect!"

The call ended.

Connor embraced Shanlee. Clayton joined in by hugging their legs.

They heard loud banging from the deck above.

"That can't be good," said Connor. "Okay. I'm going to tell Ronald that a helicopter is coming. Maybe he'll stop hunting Najah. You guys stay here."

Connor reached for the door, but Shanlee pulled him back.

"No, Connor. I'm not letting you out of my sight." She stepped up to him, placing her warm hand delicately on his shoulder. "Let's stick together through this. We can help each other. Please."

Connor searched her loving eyes. "Okay. We'll stick together. Come on. Let's try to convince Ronald not to murder."

Past the wine cellar and the galley, Ronald Jennings stood in front of the master bedroom door on deck three, a small ax in his hands. Several gouges now spoiled the hardwood door.

"Mr. Jennings. Stop!" said Connor from the top of the staircase, Shanlee and Clay peering from behind him.

Ronald Jennings tilted his large body toward them. Beads of sweat trickled down his face, soaking his collar. He was a businessman gone mad. "What?"

"We just contacted the authorities. A helicopter should arrive here in five to six hours."

Ronald clenched the ax with both hands, readjusting the position of his fingers, and then turned back to the door. He swung another blow.

"Stop! Don't do this!" Shanlee cried.

"Don't bother me!" Ronald shouted.

"Sir," said Connor, "Najah is innocent until proven guilty. She has a right to a fair trial. What evidence do you have that she is the killer?"

After striking the door with a loud *whack*, Ronald heaved a great breath. "She defied my orders. I told her to stay in the lounge!"

"That is not enough evidence," said Connor. "Let her hide in Orlean's room. We're all trying to survive. Mr. Jennings, Najah has the right to due process of law!"

Ronald turned around, grabbed a gun from his pocket, and pointed it. Connor backed away, hands in the air.

Ronald's face was horribly red. "Due process? Due process? My brother was all about due process and mercy. And look where that got him. He's dead! And we're all going to die unless we take matters into our own hands! Now, get out of my sight. I'm going to make the maid regret that she ever crossed me." He returned the gun to his pocket and swung the ax back at the door. *Whack! Whack! Whack!*

Connor gestured for Shanlee and Clayton to follow him down the staircase. "Come on. This isn't safe. I have an idea."

They fled back to deck one.

"Connor. You have to tell me." Shanlee paused at the bottom of the stone-inlaid steps. "What are we doing?"

Connor retreated to her position. "Shanlee, we are going to find a hiding place for Clayton," he whispered. "But we don't know who's listening. Wait…"

The door to the chef's room was open. The combination lock was on the floor. And the room was empty.

28

The Past

Inside the college classroom building, two girls giggled and whispered to each other as they passed a young couple on a couch. The couch was made for studying, not lounging. Even so, nineteen-year-old Connor and his girlfriend, Littlebird Jeswick, were cuddling together as they watched a movie on her laptop. Connor had just taken their relationship to the next level by asking her father for his permission to date Littlebird. He had granted it. Things were going well, or so it would seem.

Connor lifted his head off Littlebird's curly red locks as the film ended.

"That was so good," she remarked. "But now, back to math homework."

As they placed their textbooks on their laps, Connor decided that he didn't want to study. He wanted to talk. "Um, can we discuss something? Just for a minute."

"Oh. Okay." Littlebird slammed her textbook shut and turned to him. "What's on your mind?"

"Well. Hmm. This is a bit difficult to bring up."

Her eyes widened. "Uh-oh."

"So, um, Littlebird." Connor cleared his throat. "I'm kind of dissatisfied with our relationship."

"What? Why?"

"Well, I always wanted to have deep, long conversations with my girlfriend. But when we hangout it's like we can only talk for a short time." Connor kept going. "I want to get deeper, to dig down into the real topics."

Littlebird nodded politely. "Con, we've been date'n on and off for almost two years now. We know each other pretty well. I see what you're say'n. But the thing is, I'm take'n a real hard math class right now. I'm exhausted almost all the time. I don't have much go'n through my head except 'I just want to be done.' I hate this class."

Connor pushed forward with his decision. "The thing is, I don't think I'm willing to wait. We'll probably break up in the future anyway. Let's just call it off now."

Littlebird blinked rapidly as she filled her backpack with textbooks and a laptop.

"Wait, tell me what you're thinking."

"No, Connor." She sighed. "You've broken up with me so many times. This time I'm just gonna go."

A tiny potted cactus rested on the rustic wooden coffee table in the summery desert of Nevada. The loud hum of the espresso machine startled twenty-year-old Connor. He laughed at himself. He was super nervous.

Wearing a long blue skirt and a short-sleeved blouse, Joy Greenwood entered the coffee shop. She walked right up to Connor, giving him an affectionate hug.

"I bought you a cardamom latté," said Connor. "A classy drink for a classy girl."

Joy smiled, hesitantly sitting down on the upholstered leather chair. "Thank you, Con. That's very kind of you. But I have to say something. This is not a date."

Connor thought for a minute. *Not a date? What? Then it must be whatever the stage is before dating. The jittery talking stage. That must be it.*

"Okay. That's fine. Whatever you like," said Connor.

"Good." Joy sipped her latté. "Oh! This is really good."

"Yeah. I got the same thing." Connor laughed nervously. "Cardamom is the secret ingredient."

"So, what did you want to talk with me about?" Joy inquired.

"Um, well." Connor took a deep breath. Here it went. "I just wanted to tell you that I've had a crush on you for many years. Like, ever since we were kids."

Joy's gaping mouth shifted into an honored smile. "Oh."

Connor felt encouraged. "Remember that time I put a lizard on your shoulder?"

"Yes. When we were like fourteen?"

"Yes. I was really trying to communicate to you that I liked you. I wanted to date you. But of course, we were teenagers and nobody in our friend group dated in high school."

Joy took a lengthy glug from her latté. "Wow. Connor, I didn't expect to hear this today." She put her hands over her mouth, then awkwardly onto her lap, then under her legs. "I'll just sit on my hands. So hard to find a place to put them."

Connor guffawed excitedly. "Yes. Hands! Can't live with them, can't live without them."

Joy laughed a bit. "Yep. So, Connor. This is really nice of you to say. I kind of suspected as much. But I have to tell you"—her brow crinkled compassionately—"the feelings are not reciprocated."

Connor suddenly felt very warm. He nodded too many times. "Okay. Okay. That's okay."

"You're a man who likes martial arts and exploring the world. But me." She shrugged. "I'm just a simple homebody. We don't have enough in common."

"Joy, just listen to me for a second." He scooted forward. "You're right, I do like to travel. But in my heart, I want to settle down and raise a family. Do you know why I went to college outside of Nevada?"

"Why?"

"Because of the situation that happened with the Stonewells." Connor exhaled heavily. "They shunned me five years ago. And it just crushed me. I had to go somewhere else to try to get back on my feet again."

Joy pulled her hands out, clenching them tightly in front of her. "They did that because they were concerned you had a crush on Blake. They were just trying to protect their son."

Connor's heart sank at the reminder. "But I didn't have a crush on him! That's the thing! It was all one horrible misunderstanding. Blake was like a big brother to me. I guess I was just too vocal about the many questions spinning around in my head."

"There's always two sides to every story," said Joy dismissively. "Andalucía felt intimidated by you. You were too pushy."

"Maybe I was too pushy at times. But I was just trying to explain what actually happened." Connor pressed his temples as if it would dispel all the bad memories. "You guys still hang out with me. Your brother Skander is one of my best friends. Why haven't you guys pulled away? Why aren't you trying to protect your siblings from me?"

"Because we haven't been through the same situation," Joy answered. "We also see the good in you, the good that the Stonewells lost sight of."

Connor was feeling powerless. "So, because of what happened when I was fifteen, you will never consider me?"

Joy became a bit somber. She grasped one elvish braid that was hidden in the sheet of her brown hair as if holding on to a rope for strength. "Connor, our choices shape who we become. Every choice we make is like a hammer on our souls, forming us in one way or another. And you and I, we are just going in very different directions." Joy leaned forward. "I know you're disappointed. But I do want to continue being your friend. Can I ask you something?"

"Sure."

"Will you be like a brother to me?"

Connor rubbed his forehead. His high school dreams were all dead. Now he had to decide how to live differently. "Okay. Yes. I'll be like a brother to you."

The small white Toyota pulled up to the Seattle airport. Twenty-two-year-old Connor quickly got out of the passenger seat, rushing to the trunk. The driver, who was also Connor's girlfriend, met him there. She was almost as tall as Connor, with bright-blond hair, pale skin, and a very expressive face. Her name was Liberty Forester.

"I guess this is where we say goodbye," said Liberty as she reached over for a tender hug.

Connor did not return the embrace with much gusto. And Liberty noticed.

"What's wrong?" she asked.

Connor allowed his nervous eyes to meet hers. "You know, there's still some time before my flight takes off. Can we go somewhere—to talk for a bit?"

Liberty's smile faded. She became deeply concerned; the skin between her eyebrows bent like a hinge on a door. "Of course. Definitely. Yes, we can do that."

As they drove out of the airport, Connor called out instructions. "Get in the left lane." And, "Why don't you take a turn here?"

"You know, I think this is good enough." Liberty made a sharp turn into a parking lot. With the vehicle stopped, she leaned against the driver's-side door and stared at him. Her expression simply dripped with trepidation.

"Well, Liberty, this has been a good time, visiting you here in Seattle," Connor began. "We've had some fun."

"Yes, we have. And?"

"Well, I-I just don't know how we can keep doing this. You know, dating long-distance. I'm planning to move back to Nevada when I graduate in May. That's where my family is, so that's where I want to live. But it seems like you're not going to move out of Washington, huh?"

"I'm about to secure my dream job here," Liberty defended. "It's going to be good. I know it! But we'll get through it. I love our video calls."

Connor picked at the air vent. "But that's just it, I don't like the video calls that much. I like being in person. I like dating in real life. You know?"

Liberty exhaled a great weight. "I have a feeling you're making an excuse. I don't know why I feel that way. It's just this strong vibe. Are you making an excuse? What's the real reason you're doubting our relationship? Things have been going well. I felt like we really connected this week."

Connor's heartbeat shifted into a higher gear. He had never told Liberty about the secrets of his past, and he didn't want to start now. But she was catching on. Connor felt a strong impulse to run away. "I'm not making an excuse," he lied. "We're going in different directions; we live in different states. I just can't foresee this working out. I'm sorry."

Liberty held back her tears. "Okay," she said in a small voice. "That's okay. I'll drive you back to the airport."

29

At the very end of the hallway on deck one, Connor twisted a flat circular handle in the wall, opening a small door. Shanlee and Clayton followed him into the hull, the basement of the yacht. Sounds of splashing waves and the humming engine were quite loud there. Four bright-orange lifeboats were fastened onto the beams in the floor, covered by white cloth.

"Shanlee, can you please watch the door?" Connor requested, gently placing his hand on her shoulder. "There's no telling where the chef and Durand are."

"Yes. I'll do that." Shanlee closed the door almost all the way, leaving only a thin sliver as her peephole.

Connor guided Clayton to one of the life boats, carefully maneuvering around the long metal beams. The seven-year-old boy inclined his head. "What's happening?"

Connor crouched down to Clayton's level. "I'm going to ask you to play a game with me. It's a game that might last for a little while, like a few hours."

"Okay. What's the game?"

"Hide-and-go-seek," said Connor. "And you're the one hiding. You win if Shanlee or I come back in here and say, 'The coast is clear.' " He became very serious. "Do not answer to anyone else, especially Durand, the chef, or your uncle Ronald. Only come out of hiding if Shanlee or I call you. Got it?"

Clay nodded, tapping his palm on the stretched canvas that covered the lifeboat. "I kind of want to hide in here."

Connor smiled. "You're already ahead of the game, buddy. Yes, this is where I was thinking you could hide."

Clay pointed to one of the other lifeboats. "Maybe Mommy could hide in that one."

Connor considered reminding Clay that his mother was dead. But it didn't seem like the right time. "She can't hide in here right now. It's just going to be you."

"It's weally loud." Clayton dug his fingers into his pocket, removing lint, a map for a toy car game, and two bright-green earplugs. As he put them into his ears, he looked at Connor and said, "I weally want you to come back for me."

Connor closed his eyes for a moment, gulping. "We will. All right, now it's time to play. Get inside." He lifted the canvas, and Clayton crawled into his new hiding spot.

With one final chop, Ronald Jennings smashed through the door. He reached in, unlocked the deadbolt, and knocked the door in with the back of his ax. "Najah. It's time to face the consequences for your actions." His weight shifted from one massive leg to the next, the floor creaking beneath him.

He kicked open the door to the bathroom on his left. The white marble counters, walls, and floor were pristine as ever. But the glass shower door was closed with some kind of dark shadow behind it. Ronald fired his gun. The foggy glass shattered, thousands of pieces glittering on the floor, revealing a disappointing truth: the dark form was only a towel.

"Come out! Idiot maid!" He raced across the hallway to the walk-in closet. The room was a maze of dresses, purses, shoes, and bric-a-brac.

Then a shot fired, snagging Ronald on the edge of his shoulder. "Aaghhhhhh!" He lumbered out to the bedroom and squatted behind the couch. "So, you are the murderer!"

From behind the bed, Najah Hasan pointed a silver handgun, firing it a second time in Ronald's direction. "I've never killed anyone," her shrill voice replied. "But I will kill you."

"Not so easily!" he shouted. "You're not getting me! I'm going to win this!" Reaching up above the sofa, Ronald Jennings fired back.

Connor and Shanlee had just arrived on deck three when they heard the gunfire. "Oh no!" Shanlee exclaimed.

"They're shooting at each other?" Connor shook his head. "This isn't right! I have to try to reason with them. We don't want anyone else to die."

"Connor, no. You're not thinking straight," Shanlee pleaded. "You could get hurt in there!"

"I'll be fine. Stay here for just a second. I'll be right back." Connor ran toward the bedroom. "Please stop the gunfire!" He slowly entered the master suite. "We believe that Durand is the murderer. We have evidence to support this." He spotted Ronald behind the couch and Najah behind the bed. "Please put down your guns! Help is on the way! No one else needs to die!"

Najah pointed her handgun at Connor and fired, but he dodged it just in time.

"See!" Ronald bellowed. "She's a killer!"

Connor's blood raced as he fled the master suite, escaping with his life. "You were right, Shanlee. It's very dangerous in there." He sighed heavily. "It's such a shame! Help is coming in a few hours and they are going to destroy each other! What's wrong with them?"

"They're desperate, I guess," said Shanlee. "We just have to leave them alone. Oh, but I'm glad you're safe." They held hands as they sat on the staircase. "What's the plan now?"

"We need to find Durand and the chef. They're probably upstairs, on deck four or five." Connor pulled out his revolver. "I'm not going to mess with Ronald and Najah, but I will defend you and myself if needed."

Shanlee embraced Connor's left arm, leaning close. "Thank you." Then she moved. "Oh, what's that?"

Shanlee crawled up the staircase, retrieving one lonely piece of paper with a photograph on it. "It's a picture of Julia and Jeralynn Stonewell. They're two of my friends from back home."

Connor felt a shiver run through him at the mention of the names. "What? Can I see that?" He snatched up the paper. Sure enough, it was a photograph of the youngest Stonewell siblings playing two violins on a stage.

Shanlee looked at him, confused. "Do you know them?"

Connor examined the picture several times, struggling to believe. "Yes. I mean, I knew their brothers. But I don't—I don't understand why it's here."

"Julia's a good friend of mine," said Shanlee. "I met her at a debate class in high school. Her mom is really sweet."

Connor stared blankly at her. "What? You mean you're close?"

"Yeah. A little bit. Why? What's the problem?"

But Connor didn't answer. He stuffed the page into his pocket. "Come on. Let's find Durand."

30

The Past

Three weeks had passed since Connor moved back to Henderson, Nevada from college on the east coast. He was enjoying living close to his parents and siblings again. One day, he stopped by a café to grab a bite to eat before a movie night at a friend's house. He was sitting out on the patio, the sun just starting to sink below the distant mesa on the horizon, when the sauce from his sandwich spilled all over his hands. He hurried inside to fetch a napkin. But while he made his way out, he spotted Mrs. Stonewell at an indoor table with another middle-aged woman. Connor was happy to see her. Mrs. Stonewell had said a few cordial words to Connor at a couple community events when he had visited Nevada in recent years. Maybe this time she would be the motherly figure he had once known. He decided to walk up and say hi.

Mrs. Stonewell shot him a look of horror when she noticed his waving hand. Her forehead crinkled and her eyes went wide. She did not even attempt to smile. She turned away, shielding her face with her hand.

Connor rushed out of the café, fearing that the Stonewells would call the police. He felt guilty; he felt ashamed. He expected that Mr. Stonewell would email his parents, requesting once again for Connor to stop contacting them—until he realized that he was twenty-two years old now.

Despite many challenges, Connor was a stubborn idealist. Reconciliation was once his favorite word. He had told himself for many years that the Stonewells were good, loving people, and one day they would see how Connor had changed. One day they would ask him to be their friend again. They were a blessed family whom he respected. Andalucía Stonewell was such a light of life and humor, wisdom and encouragement. Blake was a stalwart young man, an example to his peers of kindness, strength, and diligence. But the hard truth was apparent. Andalucía had no interest in reconciliation.

Andalucía Stonewell had once been a matron of encouragement in Connor's childhood. She had once looked him in the eyes and perceived a great deal of budding potential to do good in the world. Overtime, he grew to trust her. But after she proved to be a stable confidante when Mrs. Alekseev was in the hospital, Connor trusted Andalucía on such a deep level that he handed over the ability to define himself. He had turned to Blake and Andalucía for advice concerning his secret issue, his dark problem. Sadly, they determined Connor to be an incurable distortion. Even though he hated to admit it, Connor had the potential for only one thing in Andalucía's sight—harm.

The encouraging words were long gone. The motherly affection was a fading memory of the distant past. All that remained was a back turned toward Connor, a hand raised as a protective shield, and a cold shoulder.

Connor's belief in himself shook. The bars of shame threatened to lock him in forever. A question hammered in his mind: what if they're right?

Connor had one comfort as he walked away: Jesus Christ believed in reconciliation. No matter how many people Connor lost, no matter how harshly his old comrades shunned him, no matter how confused he became about his own worth—Connor would always find a friend in Jesus.

Frantically, Connor pieced together a new plan. He would move away again. He had always wanted to live near a beach. Not California, though; that was too close. Why not Florida? Yes! Florida was sure to be a place where Connor could escape this wretched feeling. Certainly there, by the flat sandy beaches and the peaceful palm trees, Connor could build a new life with new friendships and a much brighter future.

31

Connor felt like such a fool. How could he believe he had a chance to date Shanlee? Of course she wouldn't accept him. Everything would have to end now. Even if they survived the *Chrysalis* and made it back to America, Connor would have to call it off with her. There was no way it would work out now. What a shame. Connor really liked her.

"Let's stop here," he said as they arrived on deck four. The sliding glass doors were right next to the spiral staircase. Through the glass, he saw Xenon Leveque standing between the sun chairs at the stern. The bright-orange distress flag quivered behind him. "There he is."

Shanlee put her hand on his shoulder. But Connor pushed it off.

"What's wrong?" She leaned down trying to catch his eyes.

Connor made sure his eyes did not meet hers. "We need to focus, Shanlee. Don't ask me questions about anything except what we're facing right now. Okay?"

Shanlee swerved around, striving to catch Connor's gaze. "What's going on? Something's changed in you. Was it the picture?"

"I just said we need to focus!" Connor erupted. "We're fighting for our lives here, okay?"

Shanlee leaned against the wall. "Okay."

Connor slid open the door, his revolver in hand. The wind whistled through the gap as he shouted, "Put your hands in the air where I can see them!"

Xenon raised both hands above his head. One held a white envelope. "I have something for you, Connor."

"What do you have for me?"

"Come out here and see," the chef replied.

"That's not how this works, Xenon. Walk over here. Slowly."

"No, you have to come out here," the chef retorted. "I have something for you. It's a note from Blake Stonewell."

"Then we are at a stalemate, sir," said Connor. "Because I don't care what's in that note."

"Connor!" Xenon cried. "Come out here or I will throw the note overboard!" He slowly lowered his hand toward the railing. "Ten. Nine. Eight. Seven. Six. Five—"

"Stop!" said Connor. "Okay. I'll come out."

"Wait, what are you doing? Don't go out there!" Shanlee pleaded desperately. "It's a trap! He's just trying to separate us and lure you out into the open! And where is Durand?"

"Blake used to be a really good friend," Connor replied. "If there's a chance that the note is real, I want to know what he said to me."

"No, Connor." Shanlee exhaled in frustration, trying to think of the words. "It's just a trap! Don't fall for it! Please."

Connor sighed and handed Shanlee the gun. "Here. You hold the gun. Stay here against the wall. If Durand comes out, then fire at him."

Shanlee cradled the gun in her hands like it was a bird with a broken wing. "But I've never fired a gun in my life. My dad was a pacifist."

Connor gave her the fastest lesson ever. "Okay, then just hold it with both hands, point the barrel at the target, and pull the trigger. See. Really simple."

"Connor, I don't like this."

He sighed. "Don't worry. I'll be right back."

Splinters from the bedframe sprayed over Najah's head, the bullets ricocheting throughout the master suite, until the firing stopped. Ronald's pupils dilated, his heartbeat shifting into the highest gear as he realized that he was a sitting duck. All his bullets were gone.

Najah seized her chance. She jumped out from behind the bed, pointed her handgun, and fired at Ronald's head. But he evaded just in time. Ronald crawled behind the couch, striving to make his large body as small as possible.

Najah laughed as she turned a corner. "Now you know what it feels like to be helpless." She strode across the room, both hands clenching the gun far in front of her. There was Ronald crouching like a fat dog. "Where are your millions now?"

Ronald dove for her legs. A bullet hit his back as he knocked her to the floor. "Gahhhhh!" Ronald howled as the bullet entered his muscles. He was wounded, but he would keep fighting anyway.

Najah screamed and accidentally fired a shot at the window to the veranda. The glass burst into pieces, allowing the violent ocean air to join the fight. The gun dropped out of her hand.

With all her might Najah kicked Ronald, pushing her shoes into his face. Did she break his nose? There was blood now. With a mighty, forceful strike that took all of her energy, she broke free from his grasp. She crouched on shaky feet as she reached for the gun, but she missed when Ronald tackled her to the floor again. When the gun spun out onto the veranda, Ronald released her.

Wobbling onto the wooden veranda, they both lunged for the gun. Ronald pushed Najah out of the way. Finally, it was in his reach! He clutched the gun between his fingers and wheeled around.

Najah had weaponized a deck chair. With an ear-piercing scream, she swung it right after Ronald fired a shot, knocking the gun out of his hands and over the edge of the yacht. But the bullet had already entered Najah's ribs.

Ronald was furious. He dove under the chair, seizing her legs. Dropping the chair, she hit him with a clenched fist and scratched his face. Ronald drew back; he was wounded and rapidly losing energy. Najah took the chance. She lunged forward, tackling Ronald over the railing. They both tumbled into the Atlantic Ocean.

Najah had never learned to swim. It took only a few moments for her to inhale the water and sink. She was the first to drown.

Ronald couldn't believe what was happening. He had defeated his opponent, but the cost was exorbitant. Would the price be his own life? The waves rose high. They splashed him in the face. He had trouble keeping the water out of his eyes as he swam over to the base of the yacht. He smacked the side of the boat and shouted, "I'm down here! Save me!" But no one answered.

Both blood and energy rapidly drained out of Ronald's back. It was like the water was extracting his very life with every passing second. In a few minutes, Ronald Jennings fell beneath the surface, never to breathe again.

Xenon Leveque sneered as Connor approached the stern on deck four, a sealed white envelope in his hands. The wind had picked up and the boat was rocking more than usual. Connor had to steady himself on a deck chair. But then he reached the chef.

"Here—have the note," said Xenon all too easily.

Connor snatched the envelope from his hands and opened it. There were only a few scribbled words on the page.

You should have listened.

Connor's heart sank. It wasn't even in Blake's handwriting. It was a fake.

And then Shanlee screamed, two gunshots fired, and Connor bolted for the door.

Leering triumphantly, Durand stepped onto the deck, a gun with a silencer in his hands. He walked right past Connor and shot Xenon Leveque in the chest.

32

Durand grinned with sweltering self-satisfaction as he gave the light-purple origami butterfly to the wind. "Hello, Connor." He pointed his gun at Connor's chest. "Wow, you are so easy to manipulate. I can't believe that trick worked. I had a whole plan B ready to go. But ah well, I guess it's an easier day for me."

Connor didn't respond. He was livid.

"Oh, by the way, here's the poem that I wrote for Shanlee." Durand removed a white page from his pocket and handed it to Connor, who didn't accept. Durand directed the gun at Connor's head, closing one eye as he raised his voice. "You will notice my art! Read it!"

Connor decided not to sacrifice his life for stubbornness. He clasped the poem with two hands and read it aloud.

> "Flutter, flutter, diamond,
> Flutter, flutter, star.
> Born by black seconds,

Great beauty from afar.

"Glitter, glitter, princess,
Glitter, glitter, queen.
Why worship binding chains?
Lose them, touch the sheen.

"Glide, glide, dancer,
Glide, glide, joy.
Twirl and hear adoration,
Smile, call the boys.

'Fly, fly, blossom,
Fly, fly, petal.
They'll catch you, enjoy,
Tell consequence to die.

"Flutter, flutter, diamond,
Flutter, flutter, jewel.
You sin but you regret,
I'm sorry, death for you.
—The Glass Shadow"

Durand lowered the gun slightly as he waited for a response, but Connor didn't give one. "Wow. You're pathetic. The Stonewells were right to shun you."

Connor glowered at him. "You killed Shanlee."

"I know," came the remorseless answer.

"Why don't you kill me, too?"

"I have to talk to you first. Someone should know how I did it. I'm a genius, you know, and every genius deserves recognition. Plus, I could use your help finding Clay." His doughy face became ugly behind the thick glasses. "I should have killed that runt when I had a chance. He is very annoying, breathes so loudly. At least he wears earplugs when he sleeps. That allowed me to freely move around the yacht and still have an alibi."

Connor prepared himself, watching Durand's every move as they stood on the wooden deck. "Why did you kill your partner in crime?" Connor gestured to the chef's motionless body.

"He's not my partner in crime! I just used him. I promised that I would let him live if he helped me. And he made the mistake of believing me. I'm going to be the only survivor," said Durand in a matter-of-fact tone. "Now down to business. Why do you think I wanted to talk to you?"

Connor shrugged. "You tell me."

"You are not a good student today." Durand shook his head. "I want you to know why you're dying. You're dying because you're an idiot and I'm a genius. You're all idiots. You see, back when I was eleven years old, I watched a documentary about serial killers. I decided that's what I want to be when I grow up. Except, I'm never going to get caught."

Connor steeled himself as he decided to listen very carefully.

"My first kill was my parents when I was twelve. I gave them lots of sleeping medications and then set the house on fire in the middle of the night. It worked. And nobody suspected a thing. I was put in the system after that, which is how I ended up at the Jennings home." Durand rolled his eyes. "Ugh… the Jennings family. I'm so glad I'm rid of them. Preston asked too many questions. I wasn't sure if he suspected that I had killed my parents. But now he has no chance to tell anyone! And neither will you."

"How did you know that I used to be friends with Blake Stonewell?" Connor asked.

"Now you're curious! You really want to know, huh?" Durand chuckled. "Tanya put me into this stupid big brother program once a month on Saturdays. She thought it would be good for me. Guess who my big brother was?"

Connor hesitated.

"Guess!" Durand shouted.

"I don't know. Was it Blake?"

"Wrong. Guess again."

Connor shrugged. "I don't know. Blake's brother Diego?"

"Wrong. This is why I'm the smart one who is going to live and you're the dumb one whose going to die." Durand sighed. "It was a college dude named Réjean Serrurier, but he went by the nickname Frenchie. He was such a gossip. Whenever we played board games he would tell me all these juicy stories about everyone he knew. Including you. He said that

Connor Alekseev just disappeared from JROTC one day and he never heard from you again. He asked Blake about it, but Blake refused to answer. Frenchie suspected that you were trying to get Blake into drugs, which is why they kicked you out."

Connor frowned. "That's not true. I've never done drugs in my life."

"But it worked, didn't it? You fell right into my trap!" Durand laughed. "When I overheard you talking about being from Henderson that first day, it was just too good to be true. I had to use it to hurt you."

"Where did you get the picture you put on the stairs?"

"I found it online and printed it out in the library when we still had internet." Durand raised his head arrogantly. "Seriously, why do you care about people? It makes you weak. People are just animals with too much to say."

"You're wrong," said Connor firmly. "People are more than animals. We are valuable beings created in the image of God. We have souls and spirits that will face—"

"Stop talking!" Durand closed one eye again, directing the gun right at Connor's nose, his finger on the trigger. "All I have to do is squeeze and you'll be dead forever. Do you want that?"

Connor became very still.

"Good boy. You better do what I tell you. Now back to my story. When Preston and Tanya told me that we were going on a cruise on a yacht called the *Chrysalis*, I knew that the opportunity for my next kills had finally arrived. That's when I decided to make paper butterflies and leave them by the bodies with poems. It's a brilliant idea. Really worked. To see everyone lean over my poems and read them as if they were something great. I think I'll make it my signature. I'll leave poems by all of my victims in the future.

"But it didn't go the way I wanted!" Durand spat out the words. "The yacht was crawling with witnesses, like your girlfriend back there. Shanlee was studying for a prelaw degree. And I didn't expect that you would figure it out."

"Not soon enough," said Connor.

"You're right. You failed. You completely failed." Durand sniggered. "I think Preston started figuring it out. He was looking at me differently. But I killed him before he could expose me. Tanya on the other hand, she was the easiest person in the world to deceive. She bought my nerdy fantasy reader act way too easily. When I was in their home, I stole a copy of *Mein Kampf* by Adolf Hitler and wrapped it in a fantasy cover. She was fooled. Whenever she saw me with the book in my hands, she would say, 'Oh, you're such a good reader.' She even bought my lie about their dog. I had to practice stabbing, you see. So, I went on a walk in the desert with their old blood hound. I just told Tanya that I lost the dog. And she believed me." Durand shook his head. "But you and

Shanlee. I can't believe you guys didn't suspect me. I nearly walked in on your library date after I killed Brock. And then this afternoon when you guys were talking about the church bulletin. I had to step out because I was going to laugh and break my cover. Don't you get it? It's a fake! I just typed up the bulletin before we even got to New York. It was supposed to throw you off the track. Which of course it did because my plans always work."

A cry of pain pierced the air from the direction of the staircase. Connor's heart leapt. Shanlee was still alive!

"Don't move a muscle!" Durand scowled, pointing the gun directly at Connor's chest as he glanced back at the doors. "She's still alive? Ugh! So annoying! This silencer is the problem. You have to get so close to the victim for it to work." He sighed. "Anyways, where was I? Oh yes, my plan. I decided, before we even got onto the yacht, that I had to kill everyone and be the only survivor. I put this gun with the silencer and some poison into a secret compartment in my suitcase. Nobody ever searched my bags because we drove to New York. I used the poison on the captain, then I went back and stabbed him, just to make sure he was dead. I didn't expect that the chef here would mess everything up and poison the cardinal. That was supposed to be my kill! That's why I put the body into a chair and added the poem and the butterfly. I wasn't going to let the chef ruin my plans! And Ronald and the maid. I saw them fall overboard from the sun deck. Fools! I had already prepared their poems and butterflies. Now I won't be able to count them on my kill list at all! But I'll finish off Shanlee, find and kill Clayton, and kill you, of course. That will bring me up to eleven kills, which isn't horrible. But I wanted fourteen!"

Connor examined Durand's every move. There would be a chance. There must be a chance. Very soon…

"I'm going to put the gun in your hands, by the way, after I kill you," the teenager stated callously. "What will your friends and family think after they see the news that you're a killer? They'll wish you had never been born." Durand reveled in the thought for a moment. "Then the rescue team will find poor wounded me in the corner struggling for life. It's going to be an easy story for them to buy."

"It's not going to work," said Connor. "Your plan. There's one major problem."

Durand's eyes shot up fearfully. "No there isn't! It's a great plan!"

"Did you clean off your fingerprints?" Connor asked.

Durand's expression froze. He glanced down. "Oh, that's right. I'll have to clean the vial and—"

In a flash, Connor grabbed Durand's hand with the gun, twisting his wrist with all his might. The gun fell. Then he pivoted and kicked Durand out of the way. He picked up the gun and shot Durand in the chest.

33

Connor leapt through the sliding glass doors, dropping to his knees as he checked on Shanlee. He put his hand behind her back and lifted her up. Her eyes opened as she cried out in agony.

"I'm here, Shanlee. It's going to be okay." Connor's stomach turned as he stared at the splotch of blood on Shanlee's upper right shoulder. "Let me go get a first aid kit. There's one on every floor."

Connor was back in a second with a hand towel and a large red first package. He removed a pair of scissors and cut off the portion of her shirt that was covered in blood. He found the bullet hole right on her shoulder.

"I think it's still in there." Shanlee's face went dreadfully pale. "Okay. Okay. Well, Connor, I really enjoyed our time together." A horrible agony took control of her face. Tears streamed down from her pink eyes. "Can you tell me what happened before I go?"

"What are you talking about?" said Connor as he applied pressure on the bullet hole with the once-white hand towel. "You're not going anywhere. And neither am I. We're going to stay right here, together."

"But Clay. You must get Clay," Shanlee gasped.

"He's going to have to wait a little longer," he said. "Right now I'm taking care of you."

Shanlee closed her eyes as she tried to endure the pain. "What happened to him? To Durand?"

Connor sighed. "I knocked his gun out of his hands and I shot him."

"He's dead?"

Connor nodded.

"What did he tell you?"

Connor held the towel securely over the wound. "Basically, he said he wanted to be a serial killer when he grew up. He wanted to wipe us all out. He was disappointed that he didn't kill the Cardinal, Ronald, Najah and the chef because he wanted fourteen kills."

"I don't understand. He was a quiet boy. I called him my brother." Shanlee shook her head. "Why did we find a picture of Julia and Jeralynn on the stairs?"

"He was messing with us. It was just a lame trick."

"But why? Why would he do something so horrible? Why would he kill so many people?"

"I know, Shanlee. It's really hard to understand. Durand just wasn't who he seemed to be. He was completely demented."

Shanlee released another gasp of agony.

"I'm sorry. I'm sorry." Connor gently stroked her cheek. "I'll be more careful." After removing the bandage roll and several rectangles of gauze strips, he began wrapping up her wound. "I need to get you some food. You look hungry," he said, trying to lighten the atmosphere.

"I'm not sure if I'll taste food again," Shanlee muttered.

A jab of fear struck Connor's heart. But he fought it. "Of course you'll taste food again. Because I'm going to get some for you right after I'm done wrapping up your wound."

"Connor," she said emphatically. "What weren't you telling me the other night? What's the secret you were hiding?"

"Okay. I'll tell you." He released a long exhale. "When I was a teenager there were a lot of things going on around me. My family had just left the community where I had spent the happiest years of my childhood. My brother moved out of the house, and a few months later my mother was sick and went to the hospital for a while. I was struggling to cope. So I turned to the Stonewell family for comfort and advice, particularly Blake and his mother. They were my new best friends. I talked to them as much as I could. I called Blake often, probably too much. I felt so loved and appreciated around them. It was wonderful, for a time. But when I told them about an issue I was dealing with, things started to change. They treated me more cautiously. One night, I grew depressed. I wrote a note to Blake telling him my doubts about myself and saying that I thought I might be a bad influence on him. His parents freaked out and I was banned from hanging out with Blake ever again. They cut me off completely. I left with a limp and I've been limping ever since."

Shanlee's brow furrowed. "I don't get it. What issue were you struggling with?"

Connor remembered the words that Norman Stonewell had told him years before in a lobby just outside a graduation ceremony. They pierced his soul like a knife pricking a finger. He didn't want to repeat the words, especially to an attractive young woman.

"You can tell me," Shanlee added. "What am I going to do? Run away?"

Connor smirked, grateful for the levity. "I guess I can tell you." He took a deep, heavy breathe, and then he said it. "I uh-I had a problem with looking at inappropriate pictures and videos online when I was a teenager. The Stonewells shunned me because of it. They were afraid that I would push Blake down the wrong path. Since the day it started, my goal has always been to break free. But-but I, uh, I haven't fully." He gulped, realizing that the worst was over. "I will go like three months or more without looking at that stuff, but then, for whatever reason, I go back. I look again. But the shame is just so heavy." Connor rubbed his chest, near his heart. "Whenever I make a mistake, I just hate myself so much. I should have recovered by now. I should be a different man. The first two weeks after a mistake are the worst. It feels like I've lost all hope of finding genuine love."

"It isn't true," she replied. "You can find genuine love." Shanlee released a cry of agony.

"I'm sorry! Is it too tight?"

She took several steadying breaths. "No. No, it's okay."

Connor tied the end of the bandage. "There. It's all done. Now we need to get some food in you."

Shanlee clawed at his shirt. "Please don't leave. Can you take me with you?"

Connor looked down at her deathly pale face. Would this be their last conversation? He refused to believe it. "Okay. I'll carry you like a little baby."

Adeptly Connor raised Shanlee into his arms. He took slow but decisive steps down the spiral staircase. Finally, they made it to deck three. He set her down on the hallway floor just outside the kitchen.

"What can we eat that the chef didn't poison?"

Shanlee mumbled something, and Connor raced out to her. "What did you say?"

"I said that the chef probably didn't poison everything," she whispered. "Maybe there's something in a sealed package?"

"See, your brain is working better than mine," he said amiably. Connor hastily searched the shelves, finding mostly vegetables, fruits, fish, and chocolate. He grabbed a couple of bananas and kept looking. There had to be something more substantial. He opened a clear plastic container from the top shelf, in which he found sealed packages of nuts.

"You're not allergic to nuts, are you?" he asked as he knelt by Shanlee's side.

She shook her head slowly.

"Good. Maybe we'll go eat over at the lounge. Come on." Connor carried her with him. Outside the window, the sky was growing overcast. When would the helicopter arrive? Hopefully very soon.

As Shanlee ate a banana, she asked, "What do you mean you've been limping ever since?"

"Oh yeah, that." Connor cleared his throat. "One time, when I was seventeen, I tried confronting Mr. Stonewell about why they shunned me. He called me a distortion. He said I was a threat to the safety of his family. And Blake said he didn't want anything to do with me again." Connor sighed. "I guess what happened is that I started believing them. I started thinking of myself as a bad influence. It's like in that moment they spoke a word over my life. Ever since, I-I guess I have trouble believing that I can be an honorable man. Maybe the Stonewells were the only ones who truly saw me. Maybe they were right."

Shanlee narrowed her elegant eyebrows. "Connor, you need to stop believing these lies! You are an honorable man! I can see the heart of God shining in you. The Stonewells were wrong!"

"But it's not that simple," said Connor. "I keep fighting myself and I still see corruption in my soul."

"Every person has to battle evil, every day. Don't mistake a struggle for your identity," she retorted. "We can do all things through the power of God. We can even be honorable."

Connor paused for a moment, listening to her as he sat on the couch. Was it true? Could he actually be an honorable man?

"It's just, they had such an influence in the community around me," Connor replied. "A community is like a net and the knots are like friendships. Cut one friendship and a second knot unravels, then another and another. Soon, all you have left is one giant hole."

Shanlee finished chewing a handful of cashews. "Are you saying other people shunned you too?"

Connor gave her a blank stare of confirmation.

"Then it's a deeper wound." Shanlee set down the food and raised her hand. "Connor Alekseev, I declare over you that you can be an honorable man! It is possible! You can be patient, you can be strong, you can be prudent, you can be brave, you can be pure, you can be humble, you can be kind, you can be disciplined. By the blood of Jesus Christ, may the sins of your past be washed away! May the chains that have bound you be shattered! Be free and be new!"

Connor felt something different in his soul—a stirring of belief. He stood up. "Keep eating. I'd better go get Clay. And the remote satellite. We should call for help again."

34

Deep in the hull, Connor carefully stepped around the long metal beams until he reached the lifeboat where Clay was in hiding. He removed the canvas. Clay's eyes shot open. He plucked out his earplugs and raised his arms. Connor picked him up.

"I was afraid that you wouldn't come back for me," said Clay as he burst into tears.

Connor patted him on the back. "Of course I came back for you. Come on; we've got some things to do."

Back on the deck three lounge area, where Shanlee rested on a sofa with Clay beside her, Connor dialed the emergency number once again, utilizing the remote satellite.

"I will transfer your call directly to the emergency helicopter pilot. They are currently en route to your location."

Connor paced by the windows, watching the waves grow higher. It looked very windy.

"Rescue team here. How can I help you?" came the voice with a great deal of background static.

"Hello, this is Connor Alekseev. We are on the yacht that is stranded in the Atlantic. We need immediate assistance. A woman named Shanlee is injured."

"Roger. We are on our way to your location. Be ready to depart in one hour. A storm is coming and we have limited fuel. We will need to depart immediately."

"Roger that." Connor glanced at Shanlee's worried expression. "There are only three survivors. But the murderer is dead."

There was a much longer pause of static this time. *"Roger. Over and out."*

Connor sat down for just a moment, rubbing his temples. Then he sprang to his feet again. "I need to check the condition of everyone on board. I have to make sure we aren't leaving anyone alive."

"Good idea," said Shanlee. "Please check my parents. But I think they are with God now."

"Okay. I will."

Connor went to the master suite first. The wind whistled violently as he observed the horrible destruction. Durand must have been right. There was no sign of Najah Hasan or Ronald Jennings, except for blood stains on the carpet and broken glass. Connor looked over the veranda, but he saw only waves far below. He shook his head. What a waste of life.

Orlean's body was on the king-size bed beneath a luxurious comforter. The azure mosquito net was punctured by many bullet holes. Connor checked her pulse. Orlean was gone indeed.

Connor proceeded to check the pulses on the bodies of Tanya Jennings, Preston Jennings, Brock Minton, the captain, the cardinal, the chef, and Durand. They had all passed on. As Connor walked away from the murderer's body, he wished he had figured it out much, much sooner. But it was done now. He wanted nothing more than to leave this floating tomb as soon as possible.

The *Chrysalis* rocked back and forth as the blue-and-white helicopter approached. The wind had picked up significantly. Connor, Clay, and Shanlee stood on deck four, toting a couple of duffle bags. Shanlee leaned against Connor, attempting to steady herself. She was still in great pain.

The helicopter swayed as it hovered above the yacht. The door opened and a man in bright red jumped down from a long rope with a net hanging from the end. As he landed on the deck, Connor saw his face. He was a black man with a military-style haircut, an edge of seriousness in his countenance. "Sit in the net! We need to go now!" he shouted to Shanlee. Connor guided Shanlee to the net. She released his hand as the man in red raised her up to the helicopter.

Connor waited with bated breath. Soon, the man in red descended once again, bringing the net to their rescue.

"I'm going to get Mommy!" Clay declared as he pulled away.

Connor grabbed his arm. "No Clay, you can't!"

The boy narrowed his brow angrily at Connor. "She's still sleeping. I have to wake her up."

"We need to go now!" the man insisted.

Connor struggled to find the right words. He knelt down to Clay's level and spoke in a voice that was barely audible above the sound of the helicopter blades. "Buddy, your mother is not with us anymore. She's in heaven now."

Clay frowned as if Connor was making a bad joke. But Connor maintained a look of grave sincerity. Clay began to catch on. "Can I go with her to heaven?"

"Not yet," said Connor. "But you can go with me and your sister back to America. We need to leave this boat. It's time to go."

With his head very low, Clay willingly hopped into the net with the man in red.

Connor waited. He refused to give into the pestering thought of being left behind. When it was his turn to finally ride the net up to the helicopter, he eagerly lifted his feet away from the *Chrysalis*.

The man in red was one of four. There was a
pilot, a copilot, and another attendant, all wrapped in
red suits and protective headgear. Rifles were
fastened to the ceiling. They had come prepared for a
fight.

The man in red granted them all headsets with
which they could speak to one another during the
journey back. Clayton seemed grateful to protect his
young ears from the loud noise, but his eyes were
growing pink. Connor held Shanlee's hand as he
watched the *Chrysalis* disappear in the distance, a
multimillion-dollar yacht abandoned to the whims of
the ocean. What a shame to leave behind all who had
died—Tanya, Preston, Brock, Captain Neals, Lady
Cavenaugh, the Cardinal, Ronald and Najah.
Connor was also grieved to leave behind the chef and
Durand. Then he remembered that he had just killed
a person for the first time in his life. He had killed
Durand O'Reilly.

"What will happen to it?" he asked.

The man shrugged somberly. "We can't send out
a tugboat right now, with this storm approaching.
Our highest priority is to get you, the survivors, back
to shore." A shadow passed over his face. "What
happened to the murderer?"

Connor looked him right in the eye. "I killed
him."

The man in red patted Connor on the back.
"You've been through hell. But you defended these
two. They owe you their lives."

Shanlee squeezed his hand. "Yes. Thank you for saving us."

Connor didn't feel worthy of the compliments. He turned to the man in red. "Thank you for getting us out of there. What's your name?"

"Ashton." The man nodded. "We'll get you back to the States. But you should know, you'll probably be detained for questioning for a few days."

35

Connor and Shanlee nervously waited at the enormous wooden table in the boardroom. Except for the window that overlooked a busy downtown city street, there was no ornamentation whatsoever. At least the chairs were comfortable.

A squat man in a black suit entered the room. He was bald on top with frizzy black hair on the sides of his head. He coughed abruptly as he sat down on the other side of the table, a briefcase tucked securely under his arm. He scrutinized Shanlee through large spectacles that reminded Connor of pictures from the eighties. "How's your shoulder, young lady?"

Shanlee delicately rubbed her right shoulder. "Oh, it's healing. They removed the bullet and everything."

"Good. Good." The lawyer opened a gray folder. "Well, let's get right down to business! You two have survived quite an ordeal. We didn't invite the kid because he is too young for this kind of discussion."

"I understand," said Shanlee. "He's waiting in the lobby. I asked the receptionist to keep an eye on him until we got back."

"Good. Good." The lawyer cleared his throat loudly. "Well! We reviewed your testimonials and the evidence you brought back from the *Chrysalis*. It looks like the handwriting on the notes does indeed match the handwriting on the homework that the inspector found. Durand O'Reilly must have attempted to disguise his handwriting in the poems, but the inspector recognized enough similarities to deem it a match. He conducted a very thorough search of your home, Miss Jennings. When we interviewed the little boy, uh, Clayton, he confirmed that Durand was out of the room most nights. With three eye-witness testimonials and tangible evidence, it has been decided that there will be no further prosecution." He surveyed Connor expectantly. "What this means is that it looks very much like Durand was the murderer, and you did indeed act in self-defense, Mr. Alekseev."

"That's a relief to hear," said Connor. "Does this mean we are free to go?"

"Yes." said the lawyer. He abruptly removed his glasses and put the paper right back into his briefcase. "You are free to leave Massachusetts and go wherever you like."

Connor and Shanlee strolled down the Florida beach, watching the little brown birds poke their noses in the sand. Clayton spread out his arms like an eagle and invaded the flock. The tiny birds scampered away desperately, casting sidelong glances. The sun shone magnificently overhead, like a new chance at a better life. Connor felt content and grateful. He was free of something that he didn't fully comprehend. He felt more peaceful about himself than he had in many years. He kept saying to himself a version of the words that Shanlee had told him on the yacht, making it more personal: *I can be patient, I can be strong, I can be prudent, I can be brave, I can be pure, I can be humble, I can be kind, I can be disciplined. By the power of Jesus Christ, I can be honorable.*

It was as if these words had replaced the definition of Connor that Norman Stonewell had spoken over him six years before. Connor was no longer a man running from the persistent fear that the Stonewells had been right. He no longer believed that relationships were a ticking time bomb of betrayal. Now, he was speaking words of hope into his soul in the quiet moments. He was changing for the better. He was trusting God. He was dwelling in peace. His heart was bursting with a tantalizing hope, new and different from anything he had felt for many years.

"I'm glad you suggested that we come here," said Shanlee as they found a spot in the sand beside a clump of grass.

"Thank you for joining me. It's so nice to share a vacation with you." Connor grinned vividly as he sprawled out. "Isn't this wonderful? We're free! We're alive!"

Shanlee didn't respond right away. "Umm, Connor, I'm going through many things at the moment. I'm grateful to be alive. But I don't feel free."

"Next time we go to Europe, we should take a plane," Connor remarked.

Shanlee didn't laugh. "Once I get back home, I don't think I'm going to travel again as long as I live."

He sat up. "What? You don't mean that! Of course you'll travel again."

She shook her head. "No. This trip has ruined travel for me for the rest of my life."

"Don't say that. This was unusual. Maybe don't go on a transatlantic voyage on a luxurious yacht again. Maybe avoid boats for a few months. But don't swear off travel forever."

A vicious anger pinched her face. "Connor, my parents were murdered! My two wonderful caregivers are gone! My dad—the role model who inspired me to be a lawyer—is gone. The woman who encouraged me every day of my life—my dear mother—she's dead! And one of my brothers was the killer!" Her voice broke as she stared at Connor with pink-rimmed eyes.

"You're right. You've lost a lot. Too much," Connor responded gently. He reached over and touched her hand. But she withdrew it.

"I'm in grief," she said bitterly. "And I'm going to be in this grief for a long time."

"But I'm right here, Shanlee. I want to comfort you."

She frowned. "I don't think you can comfort me."

The wind cast several grains of sand into Connor's eyes. He winced and rubbed them, trying to remove the nipping specks. "What do you want to do?"

Shanlee's hair fluttered around her beautiful oval face. "I'm going to go back to Nevada and resume my studies. I want to become a lawyer and fight injustice for the rest of my life."

"That's a very honorable goal."

Shanlee softened. "Why don't you come with me?"

He recoiled. "What? To Nevada? I might go back for a visit, but I don't want to live in Nevada again." Connor gazed longingly at the horizon. "I want to explore the amazing world that God created. Maybe Europe. Maybe Alaska. I have a bit saved up. I just need to find the right job opportunity." He chuckled. "I don't think I'm going to be a steward again, though."

Shanlee smiled meekly, leaving her grief for just a moment. "I don't blame you."

Clayton started digging a pit with all the enthusiasm of an imaginary game. He shoveled out thick globs of drenched sand with his hands. "Look! I'm digging a tunnel to China!"

"Oh, is that right?" Shanlee responded, shaking her head.

"Clay seems to be enjoying himself." Connor tried to keep his voice light, even though his heart was breaking.

"Connor?" Shanlee's tone was full of entreaty.

"Yes?" A sense of dread filled his stomach.

"Can you drive us to the airport? I want to go home."

Beside the TSA line at the Palm Beach International Airport, Connor knelt down to hug Clay. "I'm weally glad you came back for me," the boy said. "When are you coming to visit?"

Connor smirked. "I don't know yet. I probably won't visit for a while, buddy."

Clay tilted his head far to the side. "Why not?"

"Because I'm an explorer. I want to see the world."

Clay pointed at a design of the earth that hung on the airport wall. "There's the earth! Are you weady to come back with us now?"

Connor laughed. "I want to see a bit more than that. Are you excited to go home?"

"Yes. I can't wait to play soccer in the fall."

"That's awesome! You can use your speed to beat the competition." Connor turned to Shanlee. "Who are you going to live with?"

"Probably my aunt and uncle," she replied. And then she opened her arms wide for a hug. Connor obliged.

"I've really enjoyed my time with you," she said as she embraced him tightly. "Thank you for saving our lives. Please text me if you're ever in Nevada. We'll get authentic house-made pasta."

"I do like pasta." They pulled apart. Connor took in her face, unsure of when he would see it so close again. "Thank you for believing that I can be an honorable man. Your words had real power over my life."

Shanlee smiled briefly. "Healing is a process. But it starts with a belief that change is possible. By the power of God, change is possible."

Connor pointed at her nose. "You should take your own advice. You will heal from this grief, Shanlee. Call me whenever you want to talk about it."

She glanced at the floor and then up again. "Okay. I think I can do that."

They waved several times as they parted ways. And then it was over.

Instead of going right back to the hotel, Connor strolled through the airport as if it were an art museum. He observed the world with new eyes—the crevices in the floor, the beams under the skylights, and the colorful advertisements in the shops. He was grateful to be alive, and to be alive in a different way. Even though he was sad to say farewell to Shanlee and Clay, he was ready to begin a new season. But this time he wasn't running. He was living. The peace within himself had continued to grow. Connor knew there was an exciting adventure ahead. He just had to find it.

Smiling with intrepid delight, Connor took a sharp turn, toward the ticket counters.

A tired young woman peered out from behind her spectacles. "Yes, sir. How can I help you today?"

"Hello!" Connor greeted her with a new resolve in his voice. "I'd like to buy a plane ticket."

Acknowledgments

I would never have finished this book if my friend Brittany hadn't noted the merits in the story. Thank you to Brittany for expressing your confidence in me. Also, thank you to Kelsey Bryant Vernon for your insightful editing and having that one long phone call about the story. That helped me to understand how the book needed to change. Thank you to Plethora Creative for your hard work on the cover. Thank you to Samila Designs for the intricate details in the deck plans. I kept looking back at those deck plans during the revision stage. And lastly, thank you to the ARC reader team—specifically Mary, Tim, Theresa, Nils, Pam, and my mother—for kindly pointing out some things that I hadn't considered.

About the Author

C. R. Kelchner grew up in a home that cultivated imagination. He played story-inspired games with his brother and sister, his parents often read books aloud, and he frequently explored the Bosque forest in Albuquerque, New Mexico. The Kelchners were great fans of fantastical fiction, like the *Narnia* books by C. S. Lewis and *The Lord of The Rings* by J. R. R. Tolkien. He has written three other novels, *Lady Glimmer and the Children of Doubt*, *Life Like Stars*, and *The Blue of Torches: Ignited.* In his free time, Kelchner enjoys reading, hiking, movie nights with friends, coffee shops, Bible studies, and traveling.

To learn more, visit crkelchner.com.